Hold Me

Also By J. Kenner

The Stark Trilogy:
Release Me
Claim Me
Complete Me
Anchor Me

Stark Ever After:
Take Me
Have Me
Play My Game
Seduce Me
Unwrap Me
Deepest Kiss
Entice Me
Hold Me

Stark International
Steele Trilogy:
Say My Name
On My Knees
Under My Skin
Take My Dare (novella, includes bonus short story: Steal My Heart)

Jamie & Ryan Novellas:
Tame Me
Tempt Me

Dallas & Jane (S.I.N. Trilogy):
Dirtiest Secret
Hottest Mess
Sweetest Taboo

Most Wanted:
Wanted
Heated
Ignited

Also by Julie Kenner

The Protector (Superhero) Series:
The Cat's Fancy (prequel)
Aphrodite's Kiss
Aphrodite's Passion
Aphrodite's Secret
Aphrodite's Flame
Aphrodite's Embrace
Aphrodite's Delight (free download)

Demon Hunting Soccer Mom Series:
Carpe Demon
California Demon
Demons Are Forever
Deja Demon
The Demon You Know
Demon Ex Machina
Pax Demonica

The Dark Pleasures Series:
Caress of Darkness
Find Me in Darkness
Find Me in Pleasure
Find Me in Passion
Caress of Pleasure

The Blood Lily Chronicles:
Tainted
Torn
Turned

Rising Storm:
Tempest Rising
Quiet Storm

Hold Me

A Stark Ever After Novella

By J. Kenner

1001 Dark Nights

EVIL EYE

CONCEPTS

Hold Me
A Stark International Novella
By J. Kenner

Copyright 2017 Julie Kenner
ISBN: 978-1-945920-29-5

Published by Evil Eye Concepts, Incorporated

Sign up for the 1001 Dark Nights Newsletter
and be entered to win a Tiffany Key necklace.

There's a contest every month!

Go to www.1001DarkNights.com to subcribe.

As a bonus, all subscribers will receive a free
1001 Dark Nights story
The First Night
by Lexi Blake & M.J. Rose

One Thousand and One Dark Nights

Once upon a time, in the future…

*I was a student fascinated with stories and learning.
I studied philosophy, poetry, history, the occult, and
the art and science of love and magic. I had a vast
library at my father's home and collected thousands
of volumes of fantastic tales.*

*I learned all about ancient races and bygone
times. About myths and legends and dreams of all
people through the millennium. And the more I read
the stronger my imagination grew until I discovered
that I was able to travel into the stories... to actually
become part of them.*

*I wish I could say that I listened to my teacher
and respected my gift, as I ought to have. If I had, I
would not be telling you this tale now.
But I was foolhardy and confused, showing off
with bravery.*

*One afternoon, curious about the myth of the
Arabian Nights, I traveled back to ancient Persia to
see for myself if it was true that every day Shahryar
(Persian: شهريار, "king") married a new virgin, and then
sent yesterday's wife to be beheaded. It was written
and I had read, that by the time he met Scheherazade,
the vizier's daughter, he'd killed one thousand
women.*

Something went wrong with my efforts. I arrived in the midst of the story and somehow exchanged places with Scheherazade – a phenomena that had never occurred before and that still to this day, I cannot explain.

Now I am trapped in that ancient past. I have taken on Scheherazade's life and the only way I can protect myself and stay alive is to do what she did to protect herself and stay alive.

Every night the King calls for me and listens as I spin tales. And when the evening ends and dawn breaks, I stop at a point that leaves him breathless and yearning for more. And so the King spares my life for one more day, so that he might hear the rest of my dark tale.

As soon as I finish a story... I begin a new one... like the one that you, dear reader, have before you now.

Chapter 1

"See?" I say, balancing on the edge of my daughter's bed as I close her favorite book, *Goodnight, Sleep Tight, Little Bunnies.* "All the animals are asleep, and now it's time for Lara to go to sleep, too."

"Kitty sleep?" She holds up her stuffed cat, its once plush fur now matted and dull, a reflection of its status as the best-loved animal in her menagerie.

"Kitty and Lara can both go night-night, okay?"

She wraps her arms around Kitty and nods, her thumb going into her mouth.

"I love you, Lara Ashley Stark," I say as her eyes start to flutter closed. Honestly, mine are a little fluttery, too. Who would have thought that taking care of an infant and a two-year-old could be so exhausting?

"Love Mama," she murmurs around her thumb as I bend over to give her another kiss, breathing in the scent of baby shampoo and powder.

Her eyes open again, and she blinks at me. "*Baba?*" she asks, still using the Chinese word for Daddy that she's used since the day we adopted her. She was twenty months old then. And although it's been only eight months since we came home from China, it's already hard to remember what it was like not having this precious girl in our lives.

"Daddy loves you so much," I say, stroking her hair and speaking softly so that she'll drift off. "Close your eyes, baby girl. Daddy will come kiss you night-night later. When you're already in dreamland."

I have to fight a melancholy frown. Although Damien tries hard to be home for both our daughters' bedtimes, his work as a master of the known universe sometimes keeps him away.

In contrast, I've been a permanent fixture in our Malibu home ever since we brought Lara home. Except, of course, for the hospital stay when our second daughter, Anne, was born almost four months ago.

At first, I'd stayed home to bond with Lara. And for that first month, both Damien and I had concentrated one hundred percent on our family. Then he'd returned to the office, and I'd started to handle a few work tasks from home.

I had intended to take a typical three-month maternity leave with Lara, then spend the last month of my pregnancy working in my office in order to make sure all of my clients were happy and every project on track before Anne came along.

But I ended up on bedrest for the last month, which turned out to be only two weeks, as Anne came early. And as soon as she made her appearance, I dove immediately into another three months of leave.

Now I'm on the last weekend before I return to my office and a full-time work schedule. And even though I'm starting to go a little stir-crazy during my maternity leave, I also know that I'm wildly lucky. I have two beautiful, healthy daughters, and I'm married to a man who not only adores me and our children, but who makes my heart flutter with nothing more than a glance or the whisper of my name.

Even more, he's a man whose talent and resources have ensured that we have an amazing home, that our children will never want for anything, and that even if neither one of us ever works another day, we have the means to keep our family not just afloat, but living in comfort and privilege.

I've known about Damien's wealth as long as I've known him. Longer, really, since as a former professional tennis star turned billionaire entrepreneur, Damien's reputation is both deep and wide. And goodness knows I've experienced firsthand the luxury and convenience that his dollars can buy. Everything from private jets to personal drivers to penthouse suites in hotels all over the world.

But it wasn't until after we had our girls that I started to truly *feel* the impact of his wealth. How it will protect their future. How it's a cushion against all the scary stuff that life can throw at you.

Except that's bullshit. And as I look down at my daughter—at her sweet, innocent face—I have to sigh. Because the truth is, there's no protection. Not ever. Not really.

No one knows that better than Damien and me.

I grew up in Dallas with the kind of money and privilege that oil and gas interests can buy. Not Stark-level money, but not shabby. And yet those dollars didn't shield me from pain. Didn't keep me from trying to escape from the dark corners of my life by taking a blade to my own skin.

And the empire that Damien built didn't erase the abuse he suffered as a child or eradicate all the challenges that have been tossed at him—at us—over the years. Everything from physical assault to blackmail to professional sabotage.

But not my kids, I think fiercely. Maybe I can't protect them from everything out there in the world, but I can damn sure try. And at least they have me and Damien as parents, and not Elizabeth Fairchild or Jeremiah Stark.

The very idea makes me shudder, and I stroke a soft hand over Lara's hair. "I love you, baby," I whisper. "And I will *always* be there for you."

Always.

The word seems to expand in my mind, reaching out and poking me with guilt-stained fingers. For the last three months, I've mostly left my still-nascent business in the hands of Eric and Abby, my two employees, both of whom have been with me almost two years now.

But Monday, our nanny starts working full time—and I'm going back to work. And the truth is that I can't wait. Even though I adore my girls—and even though we don't need the money—I'm eager to dive back into my business and get dirty. I started with just a love of coding and designing apps, and from that meager start, I built Fairchild

Development from the ground up. I'm incredibly proud of not only the business, but its products and services, its growing client base, and, most important, its excellent reputation.

And while I can do some of the work from home, it's not the same as being in the office in much the same way as Damien. Sitting behind my desk and running my empire—albeit a much smaller one.

So, yes, I'm excited about Monday. But as I gently stroke Lara's warm cheek and watch the rise and fall of her chest as she breathes through parted lips, I have to admit that I'm also dreading it. Because my girls will be here in Malibu while I'm about an hour away in Studio City. I'm going to miss something wonderful, just like Damien so often misses dinner or bedtime. A word or a reaction. A silly face or a boisterous giggle.

And even though that hasn't even happened to me yet, the inevitable certainty feels like a knife in my heart.

With a heavy sigh, I stand slowly, careful not to move the bed too much. But apparently not careful enough, because as I rise, Lara's eyes flutter open, and her mouth moves in a silent *Mama*.

"Mama's here, precious," I say softly. I raise my hand to cover a yawn—it's been an exhausting day. "Go back to sleep, sweetie."

"*Baba*," she says sleepily, extending her hand.

"I know. Mommy wants *Baba* here, too."

"*Baba*," she repeats, and this time a sweet smile touches her lips before she breaks into a wide grin. "*Baba* kiss."

Damien.

I don't see him, but I know he's there. And not just from Lara's reaction. It's his presence. His heat. The way he fills the room like a force of nature, so that everything in it shifts just a little, making it impossible to not be aware of him.

I turn slowly, my own smile blooming wider as I see him in the doorway. He's leaning against the frame, those incredible dual-colored eyes reflecting so much love it makes my heart swell.

"How about a kiss for both my girls?" he says, his smile aimed at Lara, but his gaze going to me.

I nod, then sigh happily as he moves to Lara's bedside, then bends to kiss her. "Look at you in your big girl bed." She moved from her crib to the toddler bed only a week ago, and it's still a source of endless fascination.

"Big!" she says, her expression and her tone making clear that her daddy's presence is enough to tease her away from dreamland. She thrusts out her arms. "Up!"

"Oh, no," Damien says, easing her back, then handing her Kitty before pulling up her little blanket. "It's late. And big girls with big girl beds have to get their sleep. Right, Snuggles?"

"Lara!" she says. "Lara Ashley Stark!"

"Oh, that's right." He taps the end of her nose. "This big girl is Lara. Give Daddy a kiss, then time for sleep."

"Buf-eye," she insists, and Damien obliges, leaning in to use his eyelashes to give her a butterfly kiss on her cheek.

"And now night-night, okay?"

She nods, her thumb going back to her mouth. "Da*ba*," she says, and I press my hand over my mouth to stifle a laugh. "Nye nye."

He tucks her in, then stands up slowly before turning to me, a delicious grin tugging at the corner of his mouth. "Mama, kiss?" he asks, making me laugh.

I hold out a hand, then lead him into the hall. "Kiss," I demand, then melt as he pins me against the wall, his mouth closing over mine, hard and demanding, as if we'd been apart for weeks instead of just hours.

"I missed my girls today," he says as we break apart, leaving me breathless. "All of them. But I missed you the most."

I sigh happily. "I didn't think you'd be back so soon. You said you were trapped in San Diego." Even though it's Saturday, he'd been summoned to one of Stark International's satellite offices just after lunchtime, and he'd told me that the nature of the crisis was such that he probably wouldn't be done before midnight.

"For a while there, I thought I might have to fly from San Diego to Pittsburg," he says. "But we managed to get things back on track around six. I came home in the chopper," he adds. "You didn't hear it land?"

Damien installed a landing pad at the same time he built the house, and it's come in handy on more than one occasion. Usually, I hear him coming and going, but this time, I shake my head. "I guess because Lara's room is on the other side of the house."

"Good," he says. "If I take it home more often, I don't have to worry about waking the girls."

"Good point," I say, then press my hand over my smile, fighting the urge to laugh.

"Helicopters are funny? Because I know waking the kids isn't funny. That way leads to crankiness."

"Now you're being funny," I say. "No, I was just thinking a few minutes ago that we have more resources than other parents. Your arrival illustrates my point."

He chuckles, his eyes crinkling with amusement. "Always happy to help."

I ease up closer, hooking my arms around his waist. Then I lift myself up on my tiptoes and murmur, "I can think of a few other things you can help me with."

His hands slide down so that he's cupping my rear, and when he draws me closer, I feel the press of his erection and release a soft moan of anticipation.

He says nothing else, just takes my hand and leads me toward our bedroom.

The master bedroom is on the third floor of this house that Damien was building when we met in Los Angeles. Technically, we'd met six years earlier, but that brief encounter when he was a celebrity judge and I was a beauty pageant contestant is little more than a prologue to the life we now have together.

In a somewhat unique design, the third floor serves as the heart of this house and features a massive area for entertaining that opens onto a balcony with a stunning view of the Pacific. A small but well-designed kitchen dominates the opposite side of the floor. Originally planned as a workstation for caterers, it's turned out to be our primary kitchen, as it's much more user-friendly than the commercial monstrosity on the first floor.

The master bedroom is behind the open area, and in fact it shares a wall. And though we rarely used it before adopting Lara, there is another room on the floor that was designed as a guest room. It's tucked in behind the master bedroom, shares a wall with the master closet, and boasts windows that open onto both the back and the side of the house.

It's Lara's room now, done up in a cheery yellow, which is fitting since our cat, Sunshine, spends so much time in there, watching over the little girl that Sunshine has decided is her responsibility. As Damien leads me through the double doors that mark the entrance to our bedroom, Sunshine passes us going the opposite direction, her tail high as she trots toward Lara's room, ready to curl up in the armchair she's claimed and guard her charge for the night.

"She's been checking on Anne," I say, nodding toward the master sitting area, which we've converted to a nursery. Sunshine adores Anne, too, but she knows that she isn't allowed in the crib, which makes the baby much less interesting to her. Still, our cat has a nightly ritual, and it involves circling the bassinet two full times, as if searching for any possible dangers. Only when she's certain that Anne is secure does Sunshine head to her nighttime post in Lara's room.

"I think the cat has the right idea," Damien says, still holding my hand as he steers us toward our youngest daughter.

I put her down over an hour ago, and now she's sleeping peacefully, her little hands curled around the edge of the striped blanket that came home with us from the hospital. A truckload of toys and blankets and other loveys from our friends, but her favorite thing in the world is a thin blanket from the maternity ward.

I lean my head on Damien's shoulder and his arm goes around me as we watch our little miracle sleep. I have a somewhat rare uterine condition, and the odds of me carrying to term were pretty crappy. So Anne is our miracle baby, although every day that I watch her I realize how miraculous every child is.

"What did she do today?" he asks, though I know what he's really asking is, *Did I miss something spectacular?*

It's the hardest part of not being here. Of going away to a job.

And as I tell him that our little princess rolled from her tummy to her back for the very first time, I can't help but wonder what milestone I'm going to miss when I go back to work.

"Did you get it on video?"

"I didn't have my phone handy," I admit. "I'm sorry."

"Maybe she'll show me herself in the morning." He leads me out of the sitting area and to our bed. "Right now, I'm thinking of a different kind of rolling."

I laugh. "Is that right, Mr. Stark? Maybe you better show me what you have in mind."

Chapter 2

Damien, of course, is happy to oblige.

He takes both my hands and tugs me toward him. He catches me, then falls onto the bed in one motion, my body held tight against his. I laugh and protest, though it's really only for show. But he shuts me up—first with a kiss, and then by literally rolling us over to the far side of the bed.

"Damien!" I squeal when he pins me beneath him. But my squeal quickly turns into a moan as he slides my T-shirt up over my head, then twines it around my wrists, holding them together.

"I like that," he says, eyeing me hungrily. He unbuttons his shirt and pulls it off, giving me a lovely view of the tight muscles of his athlete's body. Then he runs his hands down my arms and cups my now-bare, very sensitive breasts. I rarely go braless these days, what with breastfeeding the little one. But I'd been planning to relax in the bath once Lara was down and had changed into nothing more than a shirt and loose yoga pants.

"And I like this, too." He kisses the swell of my right breast, and a hot, tight cord of need extends like a fuse from my nipple all the way to my core, making me ache with an insatiable hunger. I writhe beneath him, overwhelmed by the flood of desire that's racing through me.

I grab one of the vertical iron posts that make up the headboard of our old-fashioned iron bed frame. At the same time, I arch up, silently demanding more of his mouth, his touch.

He doesn't disappoint, and as his mouth closes over my nipple and his tongue teases me mercilessly, his free hand slides down my belly, lower and lower until he reaches the waistband of my yoga pants. He tugs the cord to untie them, then slips his fingers inside, moving down until he strokes my clit with a feather-soft motion that acts like a flame, igniting a wild passion that rips through me, from my clit to my breasts to every cell in my body.

I gasp and squirm, but I don't let go of my grip on the bed. On the contrary, I hold on tighter, fighting an explosion that I know is coming as Damien's fingers so expertly play me.

Except the explosion never comes. Just as I'm on the verge, Damien pulls his hand away, leaving me teetering on the edge, frustrated and needy. "Damien," I beg. "Please."

He raises his head so that our eyes meet, and his lips brush my nipple as he speaks. "Hush, baby. Let me take care of you."

I whimper, knowing that begging will do me no good whatsoever—and also knowing that even though he's left me hanging, the ultimate explosion will be that much more intense. After all, he knows my body intimately, and he knows how to play me to perfection.

Slowly, he starts to kiss his way down, his tongue tracing the curve of my breast, his lips brushing my ribs.

He trails delicate kisses down my midline. And with each touch of his lips against my overheated skin, I feel a corresponding ache in my core, my body clenching with an urgent desire to have my husband inside me.

As his mouth moves lower, so do his hands, until he's peeled my pants down below my knees, leaving me bare. Slowly, he eases his hand up, his fingers moving slowly over the most violent of the scars that mar my inner thighs even as his lips trace the surgical scar from Anne's birth.

I'm a cutter. It started when I was a teen, trying to escape from a life that had me trapped, the blade acting as an outlet, the pain centering me. I don't cut anymore—not now that I have Damien. But I know that it's still inside me and that it will always be a part of me.

Now, I bite my lower lip, feeling strangely self-conscious as he traces those two very different scars. Damien knows I used to cut, of course. But my self-inflicted scars feel shamefully shallow and weak compared to the one that brought our daughter into this world. "It's nice to finally have a scar that's a reminder of joy," I say softly. "Not pain."

Damien tilts his head up, and I see nothing but fervent support and love. "You know how I feel, baby. Every one of your scars reflects strength. But yes," he adds, brushing his lips over the C-section scar. "This one is definitely my favorite."

I smile, his heartfelt answer erasing my lingering discomfort. "That's because you claim part ownership."

"Do I?" He chuckles, his mouth dipping lower until his tongue flicks over my clit and a flurry of sparks ripple through me, a promise of fireworks to come. "Of what? The scar? The baby?"

"All of that," I say. "And all of me." I shift my hips in a silent demand. "Damien, please."

He brushes his lips lightly over my pubic bone as his hands move to my inner thighs, stroking up—but not far enough. I'm burning with anticipation. Craving his hands, his mouth, his cock. I want all of him. I want everything. I want—

"Mama? *Baba?*"

The little voice makes me yelp, and Damien slides down the bed as I draw the covers up over me. He's shirtless but still wearing his jeans, and now he fastens the top button before holding out his hand to call her over. "Hey, Snuggles. You can't sleep?"

We have the third floor thoroughly baby-proofed, which is a good thing as Lara has taken to wandering now that she's in her toddler bed instead of a crib. Usually we hear her through the baby monitor. Tonight, she was apparently using stealth tactics.

"Come on, then," Damien says, lifting her up. "Let's get you tucked back in."

He glances at me and I grin, loving the way he looks holding his little girl in his arms. "Back soon," he whispers. "Don't go away."

"Yes, sir," I say, then stretch out as soon as they've left the room, imagining he's still beside me. The brush of his breath. The heat of his touch.

A moment later, I hear them through the monitor. Soft footsteps. The low timbre of Damien's voice as he urges Lara back to bed. Then gentle, rhythmic words as he reads her a Sandra Boynton bedtime story.

I close my eyes, letting the words drift over me, the sweet sound of Damien reading to our daughter. The soothing tone of his voice.

And the last thing I remember thinking is how much I love that man, and what an incredible father he's proven to be.

The next time I open my eyes, the room is bright with sunshine. For a moment, I'm confused. Then I get it, and I sit bolt upright.

It's tomorrow.

And although I feel pretty damn well-rested, I don't feel well-fucked. And since I know that Damien is in his home office this morning on an international video conference, that situation isn't going to be remedied anytime soon.

I sigh.

Because right then, I really, really want a do-over.

Chapter 3

My morning is spent feeding Anne, settling in for some quick emails while she goes back to sleep, and then taking a quick shower.

When I get out, I pull on my robe and head to her bassinet. She's not there, though, and I know that she must be with Bree.

I head for the kitchen to get the scoop on my family and hear Bree's voice urging Lara to eat her yogurt and Cheerios. "How do you expect to grow up to be strong and smart if you throw your food on the floor instead of eating it?"

As I round the corner, I see her standing with her hands on her hips, her head cocked as she stares my daughter down. According to Bree, her mother is a full-blooded Cherokee and her father grew up in Brooklyn, where his Jewish parents landed after escaping from the Warsaw Ghetto.

"I'm not sure what that makes me," she told me during her first day on the job, when we'd sat together drinking coffee and watching Lara.

I don't know either, other than that it makes her stunning, with sharply cut cheekbones, deep-set eyes, and long dark hair that gives her an air of both sophistication and ethereal sweetness.

She's in her early twenties and is taking a year off from college, and she decided that being a nanny made the most sense while she figured out what she wanted to do next. We hired her when I was on bedrest, but after Anne was born, I took over, wanting to be the girls' full-time mommy. At least as much as I could.

Whenever I had phone meetings or had to run to my office, Bree would come over from the guest house and take over. These last few days, though, she's been working full time since we want the kids to be used to having her around all day once I go back to work.

"Come on, Lara," she urges now, taking the spoon herself and dabbing a bit on Lara's lower lip. "Just a little taste."

Lara, however, is having none of it.

Bree's about to try again when Anne starts to fuss.

"I'll get her," I say, and poor Bree actually jumps.

"I didn't see you there, Mrs. Stark."

"I just came in, and you can call me Nikki. Remember?"

"Sure, Mrs. Stark," she says, and grins. We've had this conversation already, so I just roll my eyes and move on.

"Oh, good girl," she says a few moments later, then claps when Lara takes a full bite.

Then she looks over her shoulder to where I'm holding Anne against my shoulder. "You must be excited about tomorrow," she says. "And today. A party to send you back to work with a smile on. I just love that."

I shift Anne so that I can see her precious little face. "Well, it's not really a party, is it?" I coo to her. "But Auntie Sylvia and Uncle Jackson are coming, and so are Aunt Jamie and Uncle Ryan." Jamie and Ryan aren't technically related, but since Jamie's my absolute BFF, I figure they deserve the title.

"See-vee?" Lara says, waving her spoon and flinging Cheerios. "Jay Me?"

"Yup," I say, moving to give her a kiss on the head. "And as soon as you finish eating, Miss Bree's going to put you in one of your pretty dresses."

My oldest daughter is a born Fashionista, and this is apparently serious incentive, as the cereal and yogurt start actually making it past her lips.

Bree catches my eye, and I wink. "And to answer your question, yes. I really am excited. But it's bittersweet, too."

"Bittersweet?"

I only shrug. How do I explain the flurry of conflicting emotions that are raging inside me, determined to pull me in opposing directions?

Because the truth is that I love my work, and I've genuinely missed it. But I also love my girls, and know I'll miss them, too.

I feel like I'm split down the middle, and it's not a feeling I like. On top of that, my emotional turmoil is underscored by a legitimate ache in my breasts, which have started to leak simply from being near my baby, who isn't the least bit hungry at the moment.

"I should go pump," I say, returning Anne to the bassinet, then heading to the bedroom to do that. I've been stockpiling breast milk in anticipation of this coming Monday for weeks, and usually the act makes me happy, knowing that what I'm doing will mean that my daughter won't have to drink formula when I'm out in the world.

This time, though, I feel sad. And a little lost.

I know it's just the emotional pangs from fully going back to work for the first time since either of our daughters came home, but that doesn't make it easier. And when I return to the kitchen after pumping and see Lara smiling at Bree, a wave of resentment and envy almost knocks me over, followed by a wash of guilt and stupidity. Because, dammit, this is my choice. So what the hell exactly am I resenting?

"It must be exciting going back to work," Bree says. "Can you clap for Mommy, Lara? Say, *Yay, Mommy!*"

Lara bangs her spoon and says, "Mama! Mama!" and I have to swallow to keep the tears that are now lodged in my throat from escaping.

"Do you know if Damien is still on his call?" I ask, fighting to sound normal. But right now I need Damien almost more than I need to breathe.

"He came up to see the girls and said he was going to get in a quick workout before everyone comes."

I nod, then kiss both my girls before making my way to the first floor. He's not in the weight room, and I'm about to check the pool when I decide to go into the downstairs bath. Usually he showers upstairs in the master, but sometimes when he's squeezing in a workout, he'll clean up and change down here.

Sure enough, I hear the pounding of the water as I step inside the large, luxurious bathroom. I can't see him yet, though. The shower is the walk-in kind, and it's on the other side of the wall from where I stand.

I head that way now, then simply stand there, breathing in the incredible sight of this perfect man and reveling in the fact that he's mine.

He's facing the back wall, his head tilted so that the spray from one of the six shower heads hits him right in the face. I know from experience that his eyes are closed, and he runs the fingers of both hands through his jet black hair, rinsing out the shampoo.

Remnants of lather cascade down his body, slick bubbles that move over the rippling muscles of his arms and shoulders and back. Damien may not play professional tennis anymore, but he's never let himself get out of shape. And I lean against the tiled wall and watch him, this man who is so much more than physical beauty. He's strength and intelligence, commanding and tender. He's honorable and strong, fierce and loyal.

And he loves me.

Loves me so much, in fact, that a tiny part of me wonders how there could be enough left in him to give to our kids. But there is. There's more than enough, and I have no idea what I ever did to deserve him, but I wouldn't change a thing. He's a miracle.

More than that, he's mine.

I watch, mesmerized, as he presses his palms to the wall in front of him and lets the water pound on him. The position tightens the muscles in his thighs and his ass, and though I'm enjoying the view, I really can't take it anymore. My body is still thrumming from last night, and now I'm about to shift into overdrive.

I untie my robe and drop it on the floor, not even bothering with the hook. Then I walk slowly toward him, trying to stay quiet. I press against his back, then slide my hands over his hips, then along the line of his pelvic bone until my hand finds his cock. He's wet and slick, and I circle him, then stroke in slow, rhythmic motions, my own body reacting when I feel him harden in response to my touch.

"Careful," he murmurs. "My wife could walk in at any time."

"She's a lucky woman," I say. "How did you know I was behind you?" He did, of course. Other than his hardening cock, he didn't react at all when I touched him. On the contrary, he seemed to be expecting it.

"Sweetheart, haven't you learned by now?" He turns in my arms so that his erection is pressing against my belly. "You're part of me. How could I ever lose sight of you?"

His words melt me, and I slide my hands in his hair and tug his head down for a kiss. Sweet at first, and then wilder. Because I need him. His hands on me, his cock inside me. Every bit of desire from last night rushes back to me, adding another layer of desperate need to the way my body is currently firing from his kisses and the feel of his naked body against mine.

In other words, I'm a wild, desperate, horny mess.

"Damien," I murmur when we break the kiss.

"Good morning," he says with a grin. "You look refreshed."

I grimace. "I'm sorry I ruined last night. I didn't realize how tired I was. You left, and it just snuck up on me."

"Baby, how could you ruin anything? And if you're tired, it's because you're a mom now. Mother to my daughters." He trails a finger down my body, from my neck all the way to my clit, so that I'm practically melting when he speaks again. "Do you have any idea how sexy that is?"

I look up at him through my lashes and keep my voice low. "Maybe you should show me."

The corner of his mouth twitches. "That's a challenge I'm happy to take on." His hands slide over me, while at the same time he urges me to turn around. So that ultimately, he's under the shower head again and I'm facing the wall, my back to Damien, his rock hard erection teasing my ass.

Steam surrounds us, and our bodies are wet and slick, and when he tells me to bend over and press my hands against the wall, I do. I spread my legs for him when his hand strokes the curve of my ass, then dips between my legs to find me hot and wet and ready.

"That's my girl," he murmurs, thrusting his fingers inside me as I grind against him, suddenly overwhelmed with the need to be filled by him.

"Please," I beg.

"Please what?" he teases.

"Fuck me, Damien. I need to feel you inside me."

One of his hands moves to cup my breasts as he bends over me, then whispers in my ear. "Baby, it will be my pleasure."

His words are still echoing in my mind when his other hand slides around so that he's stroking my clit, his fingers taking me right to the edge even as he takes his hand off my breast, then teases me mercilessly by spreading my ass cheeks and stroking his cock along my perineum.

I whimper and bend over more, widening my stance in what I hope is a very obvious demand that he just, please, fuck me already.

And then—thank God—he's right there, the tip of his cock easing barely inside me, and I have to actually bite my lower lip to keep from crying out with frustration. Because as much as I want to feel him inside me—as much as my body is clenching with longing—I can't deny that this slow torment is oh, so sweet.

Finally, though, I can't stand it any longer, and I push back from the wall, essentially impaling myself on him. "Yes, Nikki, God, yes," he cries as he uses both hands to hold my hips, pulling me harder to him. Tighter. And thrusting deep inside. Slowly. Rhythmically. Then building speed until I swear the steam in that shower isn't from the water but from our rising passion, getting hotter and hotter until we have no choice but to explode, and I cry out as my knees go weak, and I ease to the floor in Damien's arms.

He holds me close against the wall, the spray from the shower's nozzles shooting a curtain of water just beyond us, enclosing us in a warm, steamy cocoon of heat and skin and each other's arms.

"Wow," I say, snuggling close. "I could stay here all day."

"So could I," he murmurs, then kisses me again before he stands and shuts off the water. "But our guests will be expecting us on the pool deck."

"True. And we'd turn all pruney," I add, making him laugh.

He steps outside of the stall and grabs a fluffy white towel from the heated drawer. He hooks it around his hips in a way I find absolutely, mind-blowingly sexy. Then he grabs another towel, returns to me, and enfolds me in its warmth.

I sigh and let him dry me. "What time is it, anyway?"

"Time for us to get dressed. Unless you had a different kind of party in mind."

"I don't think so. I share you with no one, Mr. Stark. Best you remember that."

He grins. "Sweetheart, I wouldn't have it any other way."

Chapter 4

"He's such a little man," I say to Sylvia as we watch Jeffery splashing in the shallow end of the pool with his younger cousin Lara, inflatable yellow rings encircling both kids' arms. "And Ronnie's a fish."

"I know," she says, beaming. "Ronnie's convinced she's all grown up. And Jeffery's into everything, now. I missed most of this with Ronnie, so it's an adventure."

I glance toward her husband, Jackson Steele, who's sitting on the edge of the pool, keeping watch over the little ones. Like his half-brother Damien, he's got the chiseled good looks of a corporate warrior. But instead of Damien's hypnotic dual-colored eyes, one amber and the other black, Jackson's are an icy blue. His daughter Ronnie, now a precocious first grader, takes after him—fearless and confident—as evidenced by the way she's currently cannonballing into the pool off the diving board, over and over and over.

"You'll have some of the same experience," she says. "You're getting to do with Anne the time you missed with Lara."

"I know," I agree. "But it's weird, because it doesn't feel like I missed a thing with her, even though twenty months went by without me and Damien in her life."

Syl casts a warm smile toward the diving board. "I know exactly what you mean."

"Mommy!" Ronnie yells, waving wildly. "Watch me! Watch me!"

She holds her nose, bounces once, and leaps into the deep end.

"I swear the kid's going to be a marine biologist. She'd live in the pool if we'd let her."

Right before we adopted Lara, Jackson and Syl built a pool in their Pacific Palisades backyard. Like ours, it has an infinity edge, so that you have the illusion of swimming off into the void. Or at least into the Pacific. And I'm pretty sure that every single time we've gone to visit, Ronnie's spent at least a little time in that pool.

Damien waves to us from the bar, where he's talking with his best friend and Stark International Security Chief Ryan Hunter. "No, don't get up," he says as I start to rise. "Just tell me banana or strawberry."

"Strawberry," I say, and like magic only moments later I'm sipping on a virgin daiquiri while Sylvia enjoys a red wine.

Jamie comes running up just in time to take her own glass of Cabernet and get a kiss from her husband, Ryan. "Sorry," she says as she passes me a small package wrapped in pink paper. "I left this in the car."

"For me?"

"For Lara," she says.

I lift the package, which weighs almost nothing, up to my ear and shake it, but I don't hear a sound. "Okay, I give up. What did you get her? Air?"

"Fuzzy slippers," she says. "Sheepskin lined baby moccasins, actually."

"Oh, how cool," Sylvia says. "They'll be a great transition to actual shoes."

"That's what I was thinking," Jamie says.

My heart squeezes a little. "That's wonderful." Despite all our resources, baby slippers in the months following surgery hadn't occurred to me.

Lara was one of the "waiting kids" in the Chinese adoption system that have special needs. Hers was polydactylism, which basically means having extra fingers or toes. In her case, she had an extra toe that grew sort of sideways just past her pinky toe on each of her feet. Not a big deal, except that it makes wearing shoes almost impossible.

She had the surgery to fix it about two months ago. She's all healed up now, but we haven't transitioned to regular shoes yet. And Jamie's right. A moccasin-style shoe will make a wonderful interim pair.

I glance toward Lara, prepared to call her over so she can open her present, but Jamie shakes her head.

"We're here all day—I'm *not* missing out on watching Damien and Ryan work the grill tonight. So she can slather Aunt Jamie with love and affection later. Right now, I want this," she adds, then lifts her glass in a toast. "To Nikki. Off to enter the wild world of working moms with nannies."

I clink glasses and smile and dutifully take a sip, but it's a melancholy one. For the last few months, I've been bringing Lara and Anne outside almost daily. I'd set up the portable crib for Anne in the shade and then get in the pool with Lara. And sometimes Anne would even join us, her little face showing priceless expressions every time she splashed in what she surely considered a very big bath.

I have a zillion pictures on my phone documenting almost every second of every minute of every hour of every day. And starting tomorrow, there will be whole chunks of time that I'm not recording.

I'll see it, sure. Bree will take pictures and we have video monitors in the kids' rooms. But that's not the same. Not by a long shot.

I sigh, and Syl puts her hand on my knee, smiling softly. She doesn't say anything, but I'm certain she knows where my mind has gone. She's a mom, too.

Jamie, on the other hand, is pulling off her T-shirt and stretching out on one of the chaises in her shorts and bikini top.

"Comfy?" I say, laughing.

"I asked Ryan if we could just live here with you guys, but for some reason he doesn't like the idea." She pushes her sunglasses down so that she can look at me over the rims. "So I'm doing what you always say and making myself at home."

"Love you, James," I say affectionately, using her long-time nickname.

"Back at you, Nicholas."

"As for me," I add, standing, "I'm going to join the kids. Syl?"

"Absolutely."

I head for the shallow end to relieve Jackson. And as soon as Sylvia has a kiss from him, she moves to the deep end so that she can dive for plastic sticks with Ronnie.

All in all, it's a wonderful, relaxing day, that ends with the kids asleep and the grown-ups coupled up around the fire pit. By the time everyone leaves and I crawl into bed next to Damien, I'm exhausted, but happy.

Of course, morning comes far too quickly. Even though I didn't drink, I'm drained from spending the day in the sun, and even a scalding shower and two cups of coffee has barely brought me back to life.

"What time is it?" I ask as I lean against the counter, wondering if some genius in one of Damien's research labs can invent an intravenous coffee-supply system for me.

"Just past eight," he says, and I curse softly.

"I need to rush," I say. "I told Eric and Abby I'd be there at nine-thirty."

I hurry back to the bedroom to dress and do my makeup in record time. My hair is still damp from my shower, but I decide to let it air dry to give me a few more minutes with the kids while I brew a coffee for the road. I snuggle with Anne, then crouch down and call Lara into my arms.

"Mama, bye-bye?"

"Just for a little bit," I tell her, forcing a jolly tone. "I have to go to work. Miss Bree's staying with you today."

"Mama, stay!" she demands, her words like an arrow right to my heart. "Stay with Lara!"

My throat thickens, and I pull her close. "I'll be back, sweetie," I promise. And though she doesn't cry, her thumb goes to her mouth and her dark eyes blink as she holds Bree's hand.

It takes a heroic effort on my part to actually leave the house, and even after driving all the way to Studio City, the image lingers in my mind as I arrive at my office—fifteen minutes late because of traffic.

"I'm sorry, I'm sorry!" I say as I slam through the door that opens onto my suite of three offices and a small reception area. I'd moved from my old one-man office to this new space on the same floor a few weeks after Damien and I decided to adopt. I needed the extra space for Eric and Abby. Plus, the move fit with my plan to take over the entire floor and hire five employees by the end of the year.

I've had a plan for my business ever since I designed my first smartphone app. Hell, even before that. My mother is a straight-up bitch who tried to convince me that all I was good for was beauty pageants and being a wife. She didn't care that I loved science. She sniffed at my double major in computer programming and electrical engineering.

And when my self-inflicted scars finally ended a hated pageant career, she swore that I was a spoiled, selfish girl who would never amount to a damn thing.

I think I've done a fine job of proving her wrong, even if I only have three employees and a corner of the floor to show for it. Considering I was busy with building a family, I figure I'm still on track.

"They're in Abby's office," Marge—my third employee—says from her desk in the reception area. She used to be the receptionist for the building's entire floor. Then I hired her to work as my part-time assistant. And when I moved offices, I asked her to come with me. So now she's all mine, and she's been instrumental in saving my sanity over the last eight months.

"Traffic was horrible," I say, thrusting my purse into her outstretched hand. Then I take a deep breath, tighten my grip on the folio that has my electronic tablet and paper notes, and step into Abby's office.

She's tall and thin, with shoulder-length blond hair that resembles my own, but with more curl. It bounces when she walks, and with her youthful face and perpetually eager expression, she makes me think of Nancy Drew.

Right now, she's perched on the edge of her desk while Eric sits in front of her in one of the guest chairs, flipping through a trade magazine. They both look up as I come in, Abby with a bright smile and Eric with a quirk of his lips and a small wave.

"I have everything ready," Abby says, passing me a folder. "Status updates on all the accounts. Notes on the latest update for the Greystone-Branch interface, and, oh, just everything."

She glances at Eric, as if passing the mic, and he fidgets a bit, not at all his usual, eager self. Eric's solid on the tech, but his real skill lies in business development, whereas Abby's happy just sitting in front of her computer all day. So she's become my right hand on the tech side, whereas Eric is my go-to guy for client relations and business development.

My stomach twists a little, since I'm certain that his current malaise must mean that we've lost a client.

Turns out, though, that I'm wrong. It's worse. And when Eric says, "Yeah, I know this is sudden, but I'm afraid I'm giving notice," I drop into Abby's other guest chair and turn to meet her eyes, which look as surprised as I feel.

"But," I begin, then have to take a breath. "But I thought you liked working here." My operation is small but busy, and both he and Abby are getting tons of exposure and experience. Working for someone like me would have been my dream job when I was just starting out. So to say this comes as a shock is an understatement.

A shock—and a problem. Because this isn't a business I can run with just Abby at my side, not and build it the way I planned.

Not and still be a mom to my daughters the way I want to be.

Something like panic wells up in me, and I turn back to him, knowing I must sound like a needy beggar, but at this point I don't care. "Are you sure? Eric, why? I thought you loved it here."

"I do," he says, and I see real frustration and sorrow on his face as he runs his fingers through his short blond hair. "I swear I wasn't looking to move, but a buddy of mine—well, he told his boss about me, and I got a call, and, well, it's a really great opportunity.

"And I know the timing sucks," he says, rushing on, "but I have to be in New York by Monday. I'm really sorry, Nikki. But today has to be my last day."

Chapter 5

"Promise me you're not going to leave," I say to Abby, once we're alone in my office. We spent the last four hours with Eric, going over every single action item on his plate and making sure all of his client files are in order. Now he's in his office packing his personal things, and Abby and I are trying to figure out where to go from here.

Or, more accurately, I'm trying to figure out where to go from here. Mostly, I'm just trying to get through the day and take it all in stride. Fortunately, there are no current client crises, and if we can just maintain that status quo for the next week or two, then maybe I can find a replacement for Eric, get myself back into a work groove, and get the business moving forward again.

"Are you kidding?" Abby says. "I'm not going anywhere. I mean, it sucks that Eric dumped this on us, but you gotta admit, it makes for a pretty good opportunity for me." She grins as she lifts one shoulder, looking impish.

I smile. "You think?"

"Hell, yeah," she says. "Talk about an opportunity to make myself indispensable. I mean, I pick up the slack, and you realize that you can't live without me. I figure I'll get a raise, a promotion, and probably a Ferrari as my Christmas bonus."

I laugh out loud. "And that, Abby, is why you are my favorite employee in my tech department."

She snickers. Of course we both know that she's the only employee now in my tech department.

"Seriously," I say. "Thanks."

She shrugs. "Don't worry, Nikki," she says. "You got this."

While she's there in my office cheering me on, I actually believe she's right. But as soon as she leaves, my confidence fades. How the hell am I going to pull this off? Especially since Abby—although eager and bright—doesn't have the skill set to be indispensable. Not on the client development side of the equation, anyway.

Which means that falls on me. The phone calls. The travel. The inevitable chats over cocktails and dinner. All those things Eric was so good at. Things that I can certainly handle, but when? After Anne's evening feeding? Before Lara's bedtime story?

And what about all the little fires that have to be put out on a daily basis? I mean, hell. It's not even been a day yet and Eric has already left me with a list. Not to mention all the calls I need to make to clients to tell them that I'll be taking over their account personally until I'm certain that someone even more competent than Eric can take the reins.

The whole thing makes my stomach hurt.

I love my business, but I got into it for the tech. Because I was designing kick-ass phone and web-based apps, and had even paid for much of my college education with the income from sales across the various platforms. I wanted to keep doing that—only on a much larger scale—and I wanted the freedom to run the business the way I wanted to. So I focused on learning the business side of things, and when I was ready, I launched my small company, relying on Damien's expertise, but not his money.

Only after the company was solidly on its feet did I license my web-based note-taking app to Stark International. The product is pretty brilliant, if I do say so myself, and since it's utilized across all Stark International offices, affiliates, and subsidiaries, it brings in a nice income. It also requires a significant amount of time on the backend, implementing upgrades and troubleshooting.

I'd already intended to hire more people, I just hadn't planned on it quite so soon. But with Eric's departure, I don't really have a choice. Between the two of us, Abby and I can service Stark International and handle any crisis that pops up with any of the apps and products I've designed for other clients. But we can't take on new business.

And without new business, Fairchild Development can't grow.

I put my elbows on my desk, then bury my face in my hands. *Well, fuck.*

I'm deep into my own little pity party when the alarm on my phone rings, reminding me that I'm supposed to meet Jamie for a quick drink—virgin for me—at five so that I can give her the scoop on my day. I glance at the phone and see that it's already four-thirty.

Double fuck.

I'm sure she's already on her way, but I snatch up the phone to call her and cancel. I hate doing that so last minute, but I plan to make a bold gesture of apology. Like giving her and Ryan access to our Lake Arrowhead house—and the wine cellar—on the weekend of their choosing.

The moment I pick it up, the phone starts ringing, and I answer without checking the screen, certain that it's Jamie. But it's not. It's Sylvia.

"I wanted to check in," she says. "How's the first day back?"

"Not so great," I admit, then tell her about Eric leaving.

"Well, that sucks," Syl says, cutting straight to the chase. "Anything I can do to help?"

"Can you hire me a rock-solid team and train them?"

"Ah, yeah, no. I was thinking more along the lines of delivering chocolate."

"Well, that's good, too," I say, and we both laugh. "Honestly, I don't know how you do it. Especially back when Jeffery was so little. Yesterday I thought I'd be fine, but today it feels like I've cut off a limb."

"It gets easier," she assures me. "But never easy."

I lean back in my chair, grateful that she's not sugarcoating the truth.

"I wouldn't trade it for anything, though," she continues. "Not after how I fought for this job."

She did, too. She started out as Damien's executive assistant, but she wanted a career in real estate and she kicked serious ass to get it. And even got Jackson along the way.

"And I had it a little easier than you," she adds. "I mean, Ronnie already had a nanny even before Jackson and I got married. And he does a ton of his work at home."

Jackson's an extremely sought-after architect. And while he also has a development side to his business, that branch is mostly run by his staff, freeing him to sit at a drafting table and dream up the brilliant, cutting edge designs that launched him as a "starchitect."

For that matter, Syl's pretty flexible, too. She's a project manager for Stark Real Estate Development, and though she manages a team, she also has a ton of support and flexibility. But me? I'm already feeling like I'm locked behind this desk. Because even if I hire more people, I'll have to train them. And that will eat into my time even more.

At Stark International, there's an HR Department to shoulder part of that load. Here, it's all on me.

"I get that," Syl says when I explain how I'm feeling. "But I still think it will get better. This was your first day out of the gate, Nik, and it sounds like it was a crazy one. Cut yourself some slack. I promise, you've got this."

Those words are still rattling around in my head when we end the call. *You've got this.*

That's what Abby said, too. But do I? Because despite their confidence, I'm still feeling like a surfer on stormy seas, doing everything I can just to stay upright.

I'm plowing through emails when Abby buzzes that she's about to head out, and that she's taking a pile of work home with her. Since Marge left at five, she promises to lock up. So I'm surprised when my door opens a few minutes later.

I glance up, expecting to see Abby with a question or some bit of news that she forgot.

Instead, it's Jamie.

"Oh, dammit," I blurt, and she laughs.

"Great to see you, too."

"Sorry," I say, immediately contrite. "I meant to call and cancel, but I got distracted. Do you hate me?"

"Yes," she says, in true best-friend form. "My hatred for you runs deep." She plunks herself down on the small couch in my office. "So? How'd it go?"

"Fine," I say, because I don't want to share my angst again, not even with Jamie.

"Rough, huh?" she says, and my shoulders sag with relief. Because of course she gets it. Jamie always gets me.

"Syl swears it'll get easier."

"Well, since I don't have kids—"

"Yet," I say, and Jamie rolls her eyes. She and Ryan are still pretty much in the newlywed phase, and although I know he'd be thrilled to start a family now, he's mostly happy that he finally got Jamie to the altar.

"*Since I don't have kids,*" she begins again, "I couldn't say. But I figure she knows what she's talking about."

"Yeah," I say, but I'm not convinced. I sigh. "So do you mind if we blow off happy hour?"

She nods at my desk. "Too much work?"

"Yes," I say truthfully. "But mostly I just want to get home and see the kids."

Want, however, isn't good enough, because apparently my will alone doesn't have the power to make traffic run more smoothly. And when I finally burst into the house, Bree gives me a small, sad frown.

"I wanted to keep her up, Mrs. Stark. But we had a busy day, and she just zonked out after her bath."

"That's okay." I'm frustrated, but I get it. It's only seven-thirty, but I know well that my little girl often conks out before eight. "Anne, too?"

"Yes, ma'am. She went to sleep no problem. She's been a perfect baby today. Not a problem at all."

"That's great," I say, even though a little devil inside of me wants to hear how much they'd both cried for me. And I'd really wanted to see their faces light up when I walked through the door.

I already know that Damien is running later than I am, because he'd called while I was stuck in traffic. Now I dismiss Bree for the night, then go peek in on both my girls. I want to wake them, to cuddle them close, but I let them sleep, contenting myself with watching the steady rise and fall of their little chests.

Then I take a quick shower, change into yoga pants and a T-shirt, and stretch out on our lovely iron bed, surrounded by paperwork.

That's where I am when Damien finds me—although I'm asleep instead of busily working.

"Hey," he says, brushing a kiss on my shoulder. "Long day?"

As I claw my way back to consciousness, he gathers my papers and sets them on the bedside table. There's a glass of wine, too, and he hands it to me. I try to avoid alcohol since I'm breastfeeding, but I also did the research and know that a little bit isn't a problem so long as I wait to pump or feed Anne.

"The longest," I say, then take a grateful sip. I lean sideways against him, my back supported by the pile of pillows that rest against the wall. I give him the full rundown, the highlight of which is Eric's surprising departure.

"You can handle continued growth," he says, his loyalty giving me a nice warm boost of confidence. "But you're also well-positioned to simply hold the line if that's what you want to do. Even to downsize if it works out that way."

I push away from him, frowning as my chest tightens uncomfortably. "What?"

"I'm just saying that you don't have to go back to work full-throttle."

I sit up straight. "Excuse me? Why? Because you can support us?"

"I *can* support us. But what I'm—"

"So I'm supposed to feel guilty about wanting to work just because you bring in billions?" Dammit, he *knows* how important my job is to me. How hard I've worked to build my business on my own, not relying on money that comes from Stark International.

He stares at me like someone might stare at a wild hyena. "That's not what I'm saying at all."

"Maybe, but it sure sounds that way to me," I retort. "*Well-positioned*, my ass."

"Nikki—"

"How many times have we talked about my business?" I snap. "About ramping it up? About really making a splash in the tech world? You know what I've been working for, Damien. How many conferences have you gone to with me? And didn't you hold my hand when I actually braved Dallas to land Greystone-Branch?"

I grew up in Dallas, and that trip hadn't been an easy one, though in a lot of ways, my return to Dallas is the reason we have our girls now.

"The ocean's not going anywhere," he says. "And neither is your talent. You can make a splash in a few months or next year or five years."

I bristle. "That's not the kind of attitude that makes a business thrive, and we both know it."

"Oh, baby," he says in a soothing tone that I would normally find sweet, but right now is just pissing me off. "All I'm saying is that you don't have to do everything. If Eric left things hanging, maybe those are things you should trim."

"Is that how you built Stark International?"

He draws a deep breath. "I didn't have a family then. I'm not alone anymore."

I tilt my head. "How was San Diego on Saturday?" I ask, referencing the fact that he scurried down there on a weekend in order to perform crisis control. And, yes, I know I'm being bitchy, but the intimation that Stark International is more important than Fairchild Development grates on me. Maybe that's empirically true, but Fairchild Development is important to me. Building it. Growing it.

And right now, even with Damien right beside me, I feel terribly, horribly alone.

"Nikki…"

I hold up a hand. "It's okay. I just—it's okay." I slide out of bed and he takes my fingers, as if to pull me back.

"I want to check on the kids," I say, slipping my hand free of his. I draw a breath and walk away, feeling a bit lost as I do because Damien's not at my side right now, and yet he's always been the compass to guide me home.

Tonight, that compass is my kids, and I peer first into the bassinet at Anne's sweet, sleeping form, and then move down the hall to find Lara hugging Kitty tight. I look at her, so innocent and perfect, and swallow a lump in my throat. That's when I realize I'm crying.

Roughly, I brush the tears away, then crawl into her bed beside her, so that she's snuggled against my chest, her little body melding to mine.

I stay still, letting the rhythm of her breathing soothe me, knowing that Damien is giving me space but at the same time wishing that he'd come to me. But he doesn't, and I simply lie there, trying to let the night take me.

But then I look up and see a shadow in the doorway. Damien may not have come to me, but he is checking on me. And the steel band around my chest eases a little.

I kiss Lara's cheek and carefully slide out of her bed.

"I'm sorry," I say when I find him in our room, a magazine open on his lap. "I'm tired. I'm frustrated. And I'm bitchy."

"No." He holds out a hand and I take it, then slide onto the bed next to him. "I'm the one who should be apologizing. You're frustrated about something important to you, and rightfully so. My first response shouldn't be that you can cut back. That's not fair to you or to what you've accomplished with your work."

I close my eyes and nod, a single tear escaping to trickle down my cheek. "Thank you," I whisper.

"I want to help, Nikki," he says. "But I need you to help me too. I need you to tell me what you want."

I take a breath and open my eyes. I look around our beautiful room, then at my wonderful husband. I think about our kids and our friends and the family we've made. The life we've built together.

"I have everything I want," I say, snuggling close. And as I lie in his arms moments later, I know that I've spoken the absolute truth.

But if that's the case, why am I still unsatisfied?

Chapter 6

Better?

I smile at the text from Damien, then immediately tap out a reply.

Much. Thank you.

It's past noon, and I've spent a productive morning in my office getting all my proverbial ducks in order. Marge is making calls to all our clients to let them know about Eric's departure and to tell them I'll be calling to update them later in the week. Abby is taking point on hiring one new person who can walk the line between tech and client relations, and I'm doing everything else.

So far, there've been no crises today, and I'm feeling about eight thousand percent better than I was yesterday. It was still hard leaving the girls this morning, but I went in a bit later, and so we had breakfast and some playtime together.

Glad to hear it. Sending a car for you at five.

I frown, then tap out a reply.

I have Coop here. I drove my Mini Cooper into the office this morning and he's tucked away in the small parking garage that serves my building.

He can stay in the garage overnight. I want you relaxed. We have plans tonight.

I laugh, delighted.

Are you handling me, Mr. Stark?

His reply is swift: *Absolutely.*

Love you. (Whispers: but I want to see my babies)

I can almost picture him smiling when he sends the next reply.

No need to whisper. I want to see them, too. Then I want to see you. Alone.

I sigh and realize that I'm smiling, the stress of the last twenty-four hours fading to zero. Maybe Jamie and Abby are right. Maybe I have got this.

Sounds good to me, I reply.

His final text comes almost immediately, tugging at my heart—and at other more intimate places.

Excellent. I'll see you tonight, Ms. Fairchild. Until then, imagine me, touching you.

For the rest of the day, I spend a lot of time doing exactly that, and by the time Edward—Damien's personal driver—comes into the office to tell me that he's ready to take me home, I'm very much in the mood to see my husband.

I leave Abby in charge of the few outstanding threads of the day's work, then follow Edward out to the street. He's brought the limo, which surprises me, and I half-expect to find Damien in the back waiting for me. He's not, and a tug of disappointment washes over me. I'm not deprived of sex or cuddling—not by a long shot—but as I settle into the far back seat of the limo, I realize that it actually has been a while since we've gone out for a romantic evening. Not since we brought Lara home, in fact.

A truism of parenting, I suppose, but I feel a pang of regret nonetheless.

"Mr. Stark asked that I pour you a drink. Wine? Whiskey?"

"Bourbon," I say, since apparently it's a night for alcohol. "Straight up."

He hands me the drink and a small box wrapped in silver paper with an envelope on top, tucked in under a matching silver bow. I take it, delighted, as Edward tells me that I'm supposed to read the card first. Then he shuts the door and leaves me alone. I pull out the envelope first, then run my finger around the edge of the fancy linen stationery, with DJS embossed on the flap. I almost don't want to open it, because I'm enjoying this game so much.

But since it is a game, I realize I have to. After all, there will undoubtedly be instructions, and I carefully slide my finger under the flap, open the envelope, then pull out the card inside.

It's a simple message, and my skin prickles with anticipation when I read it:

Take off your panties before opening the box. Touch yourself—but don't come.

Then open the box—you'll know what to do.

And for the rest of the ride, imagine me, touching you.

D

P.S. Tonight you're all mine, all ways, all night.

My mouth is dry, and my pulse is pounding with anticipation. I glance at my phone, wondering if he's going to text. Surely he knows that I've received his message by now.

But my phone stays silent, and I decide not to text, either. After all, it's fun to let him wonder, too.

For that matter, I consider disobeying. Leaving the box for later. Keeping my panties on. Sitting here in the back of the limo as I sip my bourbon and check my emails. He'll know I've disobeyed, of course. And sometimes with Damien, the punishment can be very, very satisfying.

It's such a tempting idea that I seriously consider it for a few minutes. But what if the punishment doesn't involve touching me? That's something I don't want to risk.

I toss back the rest of the bourbon, feeling the burn in my throat and the immediate flush of heat over my skin. I pumped before I left the office, and I'm going to dump all the milk I pump later, just to be safe. So right now, I'm going to enjoy myself.

I close my eyes and lean my head back, knowing that the alcohol will hit me soon, and I'll feel pleasantly buzzed. And, with Damien's words lingering in my mind, that I'll soon feel even more pleasantly turned on.

Touch yourself, he'd ordered, and though the command had been on paper, I hear his voice in my head. A low whisper in my ear.

Commanding and insistent. *Now, baby. Imagine it's me. My hand, easing up your skirt. My fingers, tugging down your panties.*

There is no voice I know more intimately. No touch as familiar as Damien's. And as my imagination conjures him, I put the box on the seat beside me, then rest my hands on my thighs. I'm wearing a stretchy knit skirt, and the material is smooth under my palms.

Slowly, I flex my fingers, easing the material up. Over my knees. Up to mid-thigh. *Good girl. All the way. I want your bare ass on the leather. I want you hot. Wet.*

I actually whimper, the fantasy of him beside me making me a little crazy—and a lot turned on. I raise my hips so that I can gather the skirt around my waist, and then slip my hands back down, taking my panties with them.

Now I'm just as he ordered, the leather warm against my bare skin. And his voice in my fantasy urging my fingers to slide between my legs. To imagine it's him. Touching me. Spreading me.

Fucking me.

I gasp as I stroke myself. I'm already so damn wet—but why that should surprise me, I don't know. Just the thought of Damien makes me melt. And the knowledge that he has something wild in store for us makes me throb in all the right places.

My fingers dance over my clit, and my body trembles. Immediately, I pull my hand back, because Damien said I couldn't finish. And as much as I want release, I don't want it without him. Not really.

Not tonight.

I squeeze my legs together, squirming a bit to fight off this rising need, then reach for the package, hoping that the simple act of opening it will distract me.

I really should know better.

I peel the paper off slowly, thinking that the extra time will calm this sensual feast. But that's just foolish. All I can think of is slowly undressing. Myself. Damien. And this package is standing in proxy for both of us.

Finally, I rip it the rest of the way open. Beneath the paper is a black cardboard box with a top that lifts off. I open it, then push back the tissue to reveal my present. And I laugh with delight even as I squirm a bit on the seat.

Because I know what this is, all shiny and silver and shaped like a small egg. I've seen it before. Hell, I've used it before.

We'd been dating—if you can call it that. I'd agreed to some rather unconventional modeling terms. A million dollars in exchange for me posing for the nude, albeit anonymous, portrait of me that now hangs on the rock wall that's visible upon climbing the stairs to the third floor. And during those days and nights when I was a model, I agreed to belong to Damien.

Completely to Damien.

When it was over, he got the painting, I got my million, and we both got each other.

It was by far the smartest deal I ever made, I think as I carefully pull the egg out and hold it in my hand. It's not vibrating now, but I can already imagine the feel of it. Not moving in my palm, of course. But inside me. Because this little egg is a remote control vibrator…and I'm already on the edge of exploding merely from the knowledge that Damien could turn it on at any moment.

Hell, for all I know, he's in the front seat with Edward. Or driving right behind us in another car.

I press my legs together in defense against a persistent, needy throbbing. But I can't stay like that, I know.

There are rules to this game. And I bite my lower lip as I slowly spread my legs.

And as I reach down to slide it inside me, all I can think is, *Oh, yeah. Tonight is going to be fun.*

Chapter 7

Damien meets me at the door with one hand in the pocket of his jeans and a fresh drink in the other. He may not have texted me during the drive, but apparently Edward contacted him to let him know my drink of choice.

He also has a twinkle in his eye that hints at all sorts of decadent possibilities. He holds out his hand. "Panties," he demands.

I tilt my head. "What makes you think I obeyed?"

His lips curve up. "Because I know you, Mrs. Stark," he says at the same time that the silver egg inside me starts to vibrate. I gasp, my already primed body begging for more, but the vibration stops as quickly as it started.

He pulls me close, making me moan as he lifts my skirt, then slips his fingers between my legs, finding me slick and ready.

"I think somebody likes her present."

I meet his eyes. "Or maybe I just like you."

I'm still in his embrace, though he's pulled his hand back and let my skirt fall. Now he cups my head, and there's so much heat in his eyes I almost fear getting burned.

He bends his head to kiss me, so deep and hard and demanding that I want him to just swoop me up, carry me to the bedroom, and take me fast and hard. For a moment, I even wonder if that's his plan because I would be just fine with that. But he breaks the kiss, eases back, and flashes a lopsided grin.

"Panties," he asks again, and this time I hand them to him. He tucks them in his pocket, then slides an arm around me. "I asked Bree to get the kids ready for bed, and then babysit until we get back. But I told her we want to tuck them in."

"And then?" I ask, walking with him up the stairs.

"I guess you'll find out."

I glance at him sideways and see that he's already looking at me. "I like this game," I admit, and he laughs, then tells me he likes it, too.

We check on Anne first, and I hold her while Damien reads her *Goodnight, Gorilla* and she smiles and blows bubbles and grabs at the cardboard pages.

Lara is next, and she sits on Damien's lap as I read *Goodnight, Sleep Tight, Little Bunnies,* a book she apparently never tires of. When I shut the book, her eyes are drooping, and Damien tucks her into bed, the covers pulled up and Kitty snuggled close.

"What now?" I whisper once we're back in the hallway.

He raises a finger to his lips, then leads me to the kitchen. There's a clay bowl there, and in it, I can see a dozen or so bits of folded paper. "Pick one," he orders.

I do, and when I unfold it, I see that it says *beach* in neatly typed letters. I look up at him. "And now?"

"Now you grab your purse and come with me."

Normally, I'd expect *beach* to mean our beach, at the end of the path that meanders across our property. But since he has me bring my bag, I'm not surprised when we go out the front door and get back into the limo. But I *am* surprised when Edward only winds the limo down the service road to the beach bungalow that Damien had built for me just over a year ago.

"What's going on?" I ask when Edward opens the door to let us out. But Damien doesn't answer. Instead, he puts a finger over my lip and leads me inside.

Damien built the bungalow as a surprise for me because I'd once told him that as much as I adore our Malibu house and its amazing view, I'd love to be able to simply walk outside and then stroll along the beach. And because Damien spoils me mercilessly, soon enough, a small bungalow appeared on our property... And it was nestled right on the beach.

It's a charming little two-bedroom property, the best feature of which is its patio, which boasts two levels. A traditional patio off the back door runs the length of the house and curves around to the front door. It offers an amazing view of the beach and the Pacific, and also has a set of stairs leading down to the sand, as well as a small, free-standing shower and footbath so that the beach doesn't have to come into the house with us.

But it's the second level that is truly exceptional, because it's a rooftop patio. It's superbly designed, with areas for both shade and sun, but what I like best is that if you're stretched out on one of the oversized chaise lounges, you can't see the beach at all. Just an infinity of wide-open ocean. It's like being on a magic carpet and escaping from everything, even if only for a little while.

There's where Damien takes me now, forgoing entering the house at all. Instead, we walk along the lower patio to the stairs leading up to the roof. There, I'm greeted by a bottle of champagne chilling on ice and a bowl of strawberries.

I tug him to a stop and slide into his arms. "When did you pull this together?"

"I just snapped my fingers," he says. "I have magic powers, you know."

I laugh, mostly because sometimes it seems like that's true.

"But I think you're trying to get me drunk. Bourbon. Champagne. You know I—"

He shuts me up with a kiss so intense that my knees go weak, and he scoops me up and carries me to the chaise. "Yes, wife of mine, I intend to get you a little drunk. Or maybe a lot drunk. The baby will do just fine on the milk you've stored."

I grin. "In that case, I think I'd like some champagne."

He pours me some, and as I'm sipping it, I feel the slightest of rumbles in my core. I close my eyes and tilt my head back against the cushion as Damien slowly ramps up the vibrations of that delightful little bullet inside me.

My skirt has no zipper. Just a wide, stretchy band at the waist. Now I feel the cushion shift as Damien sits next to me. His fingers hook under the band as he tugs the skirt down over my hips, then tosses it onto a nearby chair.

The patio is somewhat shielded from the wind by a glass barrier that surrounds the area, but I can still feel the chill, and it feels exceptional against my overheated skin. Slowly, he trails the fingers of one hand up my inner thighs, barely stroking my sex as I tremble and gasp at the flurry of sensations threatening to sweep me away.

His hand continues upward, and he pulls my top off, leaving me in a lacy bra. Then he kisses his way back down my abdomen, slowly decreasing the vibe inside me until it's completely turned off by the time his tongue flicks lightly over my clit.

I make a soft noise of protest and he chuckles, then lifts his head, stands, and holds out a hand to urge me to my feet.

I hesitate, because I'm honestly not sure my legs have the strength to stand, but then I let him pull me up, and I walk with him to the glass barrier that faces the ocean. He stands behind me, unfastens my bra, then lets it drop to the floor.

"Close your eyes," he says, and although I'm standing at the edge of my roof, completely naked, the wind caressing me and the sound of the waves crashing in my ears, I do exactly as he says.

"Someone could see," I murmur as he pulls me close so that my bare ass brushes his clothes.

"Then they're lucky, because you're beautiful. But no one will."

I know he's right. The beach is technically public, but it's also very secluded, and the property is such that we're a long way from our neighbors. And maybe I'd be uncomfortable if it was more likely that we'd be seen, but right now, I can't deny that it feels exciting and wonderful to be standing naked under the sky with Damien like this.

"Touch me," I beg. "Please, Damien. Please, fuck me."

"Is that what you want?" he murmurs, his hands roaming over

me. My breasts, my hips, my thighs. "Are you sure?"

"Yes," I whisper. "Please."

"Mmm." One hand slides up until he is cupping my neck, right under my chin. The other slides down until his palm cups my sex, his fingers slipping inside me, pushing the egg even deeper. My knees go weak, and as I start to sag, the pressure on my throat increases. I'm not scared—how could I be with Damien?—but there's an aspect of danger to this that we've never played with before. And when his mouth brushes my ear and he whispers, "Mine," I feel a flood of desire run through me that almost knocks me over.

And when he slides his fingers out long enough to find the switch that triggers the egg, I really do start to fall. Damien, however, is right there to hold me up. "I've got you," he says, one hand still tight around my neck and the other steadying me at the waist. "Watch the water, baby," he says as the vibrator ramps up again, sending waves through my body that seem to come in time with the movement of the Pacific.

His lips brush my bare shoulder, and his hand returns to cup me. With the tip of his forefinger, he circles my clit, coming close, but never quite taking me all the way. And all the while he's holding my throat, just tight enough that I feel the pressure as I gasp with pleasure.

"Do you trust me, baby?" he asks as he strokes and teases me, taking me right to the edge.

"Of course." I have to fight to get the words out. Talking really isn't on my agenda right now. Besides, it's not like he needs to ask. I may not know what he has in mind, but I trust Damien with my life, my body, my heart.

He doesn't answer, but I hear a low noise of approval. At the same time, I feel a tug between my legs and then the slick sensation of the egg sliding out of me. As it does, Damien tightens his grip on my throat as he arches my body back, so that I'm the most vulnerable at the same time the vibrating egg leaves my body.

The sensation is amazing, all the more so because of the way Damien is holding me. But when he tightens his grip at the same time he skims the egg over my clit, I break completely apart. A wave of ecstasy crashes over me, seeming to last forever as my body struggles to come back together even while I try to draw a cohesive breath.

When the last vibrations of the orgasm pass, Damien scoops me up. He has no choice, really, because my legs are essentially nonfunctional at this point. He carries me back to the chaise and lays me down as I keep my arms hooked around his neck.

"Please," I murmur. "Don't make me beg."

He kisses my nose. "I like it when you beg. But right now, I can't wait any longer." Gently, he pulls back, forcing me to either rise with him or to release him. I choose the latter, letting my fingers graze his face, tracing over the light scruff of his evening beard as he straightens and I sink back into the cushion.

I watch as he strips off his clothes. His shirt falling to the ground. His jeans sliding over his hips. His gray boxer briefs easing down to free his cock, which is hard and huge and ready.

For a moment he just stands there, and I gaze greedily at him, this man who belongs to me. The sun is sinking low in the sky, casting an orange glow over the patio and illuminating Damien's skin. I can imagine him as a sculptor's model, his image carved in marble forever.

But it's not his beauty that I crave, it's what's inside him. I want the man who loves me. Who makes me laugh and makes me feel safe. The man who is the father of my children, and who will always—*always*—watch over us.

I hold out my hands in a silent demand, and he comes to me, easing up the chaise between my now-spread legs. "Make love to me," I whisper, then melt a little when he says "Nikki" with such tenderness that his voice feels like a caress.

He kisses me, feather-light at first, but then harder and more demanding, and I cling to him, my hands tight on his shoulders. I want him inside me, to feel the connection, so deep that I don't know where I end and he begins. And I hook my legs over his, easing them higher until I'm gripping him with my thighs, and his cock is right at my center, and I'm open and wet and so completely ready.

"Damien," I demand, squirming against him as I close my eyes and soak in the feel of him. "Now. Please, please, now."

"Look at me," he says, and I open my eyes, only to see so much heat and longing and intensity reflected back at me that I would swear he was already inside me. I feel my core tighten, clenching and unclenching in a silent demand. And when he shifts just enough so that he barely slips inside me, I gasp from the sensation of being entered—and in anticipation of being filled.

"Now," he says, his eyes still on mine. And in time with the word, he pistons his hips, thrusting inside of me, and then going deeper and deeper with each slow, mesmerizing thrust.

Gradually, he speeds up, our combined passion fueling a need. Until finally, he's pounding inside me, thrusting me back against the chaise as I cling even tighter, certain that somehow he's going to fuck me so hard that we're going to actually meld into one person.

"Touch yourself, baby. I want to feel you explode."

I'm so close, and I do as he says, taking one hand off his back and sliding it between our bodies so that I can stroke my clit as he thrusts inside me, until the melding of the sensations is too much to bear and I feel an electrical prickling on my inner thighs, a signal of a coming orgasm.

"Damien," I beg as I stroke myself, desperate now to go over that edge. "Please," I add, though I'm not even sure what I'm asking.

But as my body starts to shake—as I arch up and cry out as millions of electric sparks race over my body—I know that I was demanding that he come with me. And now my body is milking him, clenching tight around his cock again and again, in the throes of a massive orgasm.

Above me, I see the storm on Damien's face, a raw, wild pleasure that fades into an expression of pure adoration when the orgasm passes and his body relaxes.

"Hi," he says when we can both breathe again. He slowly lowers himself, then settles next to me, using a nearby napkin to gently clean me up.

"Hi, yourself." I curl up next to him, wanting both his touch and his warmth. After a moment, he eases off the chaise, then returns with one of the blankets we keep in a waterproof trunk by the door. He carefully covers me, making sure I'm all tucked in, then joins me again, pulling me close so that I'm snuggled against his chest.

"Warm?" he asks.

"Mmm-hmm."

"I thought we could lie here for just a little bit, relaxing and watching the stars."

I prop myself up enough to see him. "I think you're pampering me, Mr. Stark."

"You could call it that," he says.

"What would you call it?"

"Being."

I shift, confused, and pull myself all the way upright, the blanket falling off in the process. "What are you talking about?"

"You," he says simply as his hands roam my naked skin, making it hard to concentrate on his words.

"You're going to have to give me more to go on."

He chuckles, then sits up, pulling the lever on the chaise so that we have a back rest. He draws me toward him again, then pulls the blanket back to cover us. "You've spent months being a mom," he says. "And a wife. And a business owner. All of which are wonderful and important."

"But?" I ask, because he's clearly going somewhere with this.

"But it's been a long time since you've had the chance to just *be*. So that's what tonight is for, baby. To simply enjoy the night and each other. To just be Nikki and Damien."

"Thank you," I say, my heart swelling from the sweetness of the sentiment, and from the knowledge that he's arranged all of this to take care of me.

We stay like that for a while—our fingers twined, our bodies touching—until Damien gets up, telling me to wait while he goes inside to get something.

He's back in less than five minutes, a paper bag in his hand. "Pick one," he says as I sit up, already smiling.

"Again?"

He shakes the bag at me in silent demand, and I laugh but comply. When I unfold it, I read it to Damien. "Dinner. Hmmm," I add.

"What?"

"Just thinking," I say.

"Always dangerous. What were you thinking?"

"About those slips of paper." I make a fast grab for the bag, but he pulls it away from me and sets it out of reach on a table behind us. "I'm thinking that if I draw another note, it'll say dinner, too." And then, just to prove my point, I make another lunge toward the sack.

This time, Damien grabs my wrists and pulls me up for a gentle kiss, topped off with a sharp bite to my lip and an equally sharp smack on my rear. "Don't even think about it."

But I know I'm right, and I grin happily as I hold him close. "Thank you for planning a wonderful date."

"You're welcome," he says. "But it's not over yet."

"I know. I'm just telling my husband—" I cut myself off with a frown because my phone is chiming an incoming call, using the ringtone I designated for Abby.

I meet Damien's eyes, hating the fact that I need to grab it. I see the disappointment in his eyes, too, but he nods, and I leave his arms to go find my phone in my small handbag.

I miss the call, but before I can check to see if she left a voicemail, a text comes through: *SOS. Crisis with Greystone-Branch. Can you come to the office?*

Damien is standing behind me, and when I turn to meet his eyes, I see the heat fading to an all-business demeanor. A cold wave of regret washes over me. But what can I do? Greystone-Branch is my biggest client next to Stark International, and having them on my roster upped the prestige of Fairchild Development considerably.

So I do the only thing I can do—I text back, *On my way.*

Chapter 8

I yawn and lean back in my desk chair. Behind me, the sky in Studio City is already bright, morning having come and gone while Abby and I have been holed up here in my office.

We've spent the night hunched over our computers, trying frantically to clean up a mess of malicious code left by a disgruntled ex-Greystone employee, and to plug all possible holes so nothing like this could happen again.

But we've managed. And as I take a long sip of my coffee, I give myself a few moments to bask. This particular crisis couldn't have been foreseen, and only a limited number of people have the skill set to pull off that type of sabotage. So Abby and I had faced something unexpected and rare, and we've come out victorious.

More than victorious, really, since we've prevented further attacks of that nature.

And that, I think, is pretty damn cool.

"You did great," I tell her, as she returns from the break room with her own mug of coffee. "Let's lock this place up, get out of here, and call it a day."

"You sure?"

"Absolutely." I glance at the clock. "If I hurry, I can get home before Bree takes the girls to Lara's very first Gymboree class. And after that, I can take the world's longest nap. You should do the same.

The nap," I clarify. "Not Gymboree."

She laughs, but then turns serious. "I'm sorry I couldn't handle it on my own. I know you were having a night out."

"Don't be ridiculous," I say. "You never have to feel bad about bothering me during a crisis. Especially a crisis involving my business. But," I add, "for the record, I think you could have handled it just fine if I hadn't been around."

"Yeah?"

"Absolutely. You did great. You held the client's hand. You worked the problem. You were ferocious in writing the new code and getting it uploaded. I was a hundred percent impressed."

Her cheeks turn pink as she smiles. "Thank you."

"You're welcome," I say. "Now go home."

She scurries out, as if afraid I might change my mind. No chance of that—I want too badly to see my kids.

After Edward dropped me off in the limo last night, Damien had offered to stay with me and help, but I'd sent him home. I don't go with him for a crisis at Stark International. And besides, if we weren't getting to enjoy our date, at least one of us should be enjoying our kids.

Which means that Coop is still in the garage where I left him yesterday, and I hurry to him, sending a text to Damien as I walk to let him know that I'm done and heading home.

Then I climb into Coop, whip out of the garage, and push that Mini to the max as I race from Studio City back home to Malibu. I check the clock obsessively as I drive, and I have to remind myself not to be reckless and jump lights or zip back and forth between lanes. Maybe it would buy me a minute or two, but the idea is to get home to my kids, not to end up with a mangled car. Or worse.

Still, I'm anxious for the entire drive, and it's only when I turn onto our street with five minutes to spare that I relax. *I made it.*

I race through the gate, waving to our guard as I pass, then avoid the garage, instead skidding to a stop on the circular drive, right in front of the entrance.

I hurry inside, calling out, "Mommy's home!" But I'm greeted only with silence.

I frown, then trot up the stairs to the third floor, calling for Bree as I do.

It's only when I reach the kitchen and see that the kids' snack bag is gone that I allow myself to believe what I've already figured out—that Bree took the kids early. That no one is home.

Like Damien, I've now missed one of the "firsts" for our kids. Just a children's class, sure. But I wanted to hold Lara's hand. To stand beside her when they make balls bounce on the parachute and walk in a circle in time to music, or all the other stuff that the director told me about when I signed up for the class.

I'll take her next time. And the time after that. But even if I take her to every class from here on out—even if I take Anne to her very first one when she's two—I've missed *this* first. And I can't ever get that back.

I sigh, then drop into one of the chairs at the small kitchen table. For a moment, I consider following them, but I'd end up arriving late, and I don't want to be *that* mom. The one who interrupts class and disrupts all the kids.

So instead, I just sit here in the quiet, empty house. No kids. No Damien. No Bree. Even Gregory is gone, the valet who's been with Damien for years and now serves as a butler and everything kind of guy. His sister in Connecticut is ill, and he flew out a week ago.

"Just me and you," I say to Sunshine, who's wandered in for kibble. But even she's not interested in me. She comes for one single pat on the head, then trots away, presumably to find a sunny spot in which to curl up and sleep.

I feel much the same way.

I'm still in my clothes from last night, and I feel grungy and achy. I want sleep, but I want a shower more, and so I head to the master bath, stripping off my clothes as I go. I turn the shower on full blast, the heat cranked up almost to scalding, and I let the room fill with steam.

I adjust the temperature back to tolerable, then step in, tilting my face up toward the spray as I lean against the tile wall and let the water sluice over me, washing away the day, my troubles, my mistakes, my disappointments.

Except even the hottest shower can't do that, and as I stand there—the water pounding down on me—the hard, cold truth hits me. It just flat out hits me.

It's not the firsts that matter, it's the moments. Little moments that make up a life. And I missed countless moments in the last twenty-four hours alone. And not only moments with my kids, but with my husband.

I missed a night out with Damien.

I missed an afternoon with my kids.

How many smiles have there been? New toys? New discoveries.

That impish grin when Lara crawls sneakily up to attack Sunshine.

Anne's expression of wide-eyed wonder when the light makes a rainbow through the window. Or her gurgle of delight when she strokes the cat's fluffy tail.

So many moments I want to witness. So many that I'm going to miss.

I've known it, of course. But now the weight of that reality seems too heavy to bear, and I sink down and drop my face to my knees and let my tears flow as the water beats down on me.

That's where I am when Damien finds me, his urgent voice pulling me back to the moment.

"Did you cut? Dammit, Nikki—did you cut?"

He's holding my hands, crouched in the shower beside me as the water soaks his clothes.

"No," I say. "Damien, you're drenched."

"What's going on? Goddammit, Nikki, talk to me."

The fear in his voice breaks my heart, and I squeeze his hands as I look deep into his eyes. "I didn't cut. I swear. Honestly, it didn't even occur to me."

His gaze skims over me, hunched up on the floor of the shower, and I can see the disbelief in his eyes.

"I promise. Please, turn off the water. I'm fine. I love you, and I'm fine."

He hesitates but does as I ask, then gets two warm, fluffy towels from the drawer. He wraps one around me, then peels off his clothes, leaving them in a wet pile on the floor of the stall.

When he's dry and the towel is twisted around his hips, he holds out his hand to help me up. I take it, then let him lead the way into the bedroom, trading my towel for my snuggly robe along the way.

"All right," he says once we're both in robes and sitting on the bed. "What happened?"

I give him the rundown of the crisis at Greystone-Branch. "Abby was amazing," I say. "Smart and focused. I couldn't have been more impressed."

"You hired good people."

I shrug. "Eric left."

"That's the risk you take with good people."

I nod but brush it off. We've gotten too far off topic. "The point is that I came home exhausted. But even on no sleep and completely drained, I wanted to make it in time for Gymboree."

"Lara's first class." There's a wistful note to his voice, and I realize that he's gone this same road, too.

I take his hand, then nod. "I wanted to be there. But I missed it. Bree left earlier than I expected. And I just missed it."

I press my lips together, determined not to cry again. When I'm certain I'm in the clear, I say, "That's it. Just sadness. And exhaustion. But no cutting. Not even an inkling of a smidgeon of a thought about a blade. I promise."

The relief on his face is palpable, and I know that I've finally convinced him. "I need to sleep now," I say. "But why are you here? The house was empty when I got home."

"I got your text," he says. "And since I have a meeting soon in Santa Monica, I thought I'd come home and see my wife. But I need to go now." He strokes my cheek. "Are you sure you're okay? Do I need to reschedule my meeting?"

"No—no, seriously, I'm fine." I take a deep breath, then smile. "Honestly, right now I'm feeling steadier than I have in days."

And it's true. Unexpected, maybe. But true.

Damien's brow furrows, and I can tell he's uncertain. "You're thinking about something," he finally says.

"I am," I agree. "I'm thinking I desperately need a nap."

What I don't say is that I think I've made a decision, but I have to figure it out for myself before I can tell him. And right now, it's all still a blur in my head, everything mixed up together. Work. Damien. The kids. Even the fact that I didn't want to cut. That I didn't even think about it.

The tangle of thoughts reminds me of the code that Abby and I attacked. All the bad stuff had been twined together with the good, so we had to hack carefully to get to the core. But when we finally got that one essential thread, the rest was easy.

That's what I need, I think.

Right now, I need to find the core thread inside of me.

Chapter 9

The sun is low in the sky when I wake from my nap to the sound of Lara giggling outside. Damien's left the doors to the balcony open, and her sweet laughter is floating in with the ocean breeze.

I'd changed into sweats and a T-shirt before lying down, and now I pad barefoot to the balcony, which has a view of a portion of the pool deck and a grassy area that had been wild with ground cover before the kids, but which we'd had landscaped during the months that we were waiting for our travel authorization to go to China.

Now, it has a neatly manicured lawn, a sandbox, and a toddler-friendly playscape.

Right now, Damien is wearing Anne in a baby sling as he pushes Lara on the rocking horse swing.

She's holding on tight and alternating between squeals and cries of "Geep!", which I'm assuming means *giddy-up*.

Now she turns toward me, and I wave, then blow her a kiss.

"Mama! Mama! Come here, Mama!"

Since I can hardly turn down an invitation like that, I wave again, then yell that I'll be down soon. That I just have a couple of things to take care of first.

Since it's cool outside now, I head first to the closet for some canvas flats and a light hoodie, then go back toward the door, planning to take the outdoor stairs down to the first level.

I don't make it back that quickly, though. Instead, I'm waylaid by one of the framed photographs on the bureau. Tears prick my eyes as I pick it up, a silver-framed picture of me and a dark-haired girl, six years older, with mischievous eyes and a quick smile. *My sister, Ashley Anne Fairchild Price.*

"I miss you," I whisper to the girl who'd also been my best friend. I'd thought she was so lucky when my mother had given her a pass on the pageant circuit because she simply didn't win. I'd been so envious—hating every crown I earned and wanting nothing more than to have time and food and my mother's love that didn't come with strings. Especially since those strings were the threads of pageant gowns.

I'd thought that Ashley had escaped my mother and her belief that everything—and everyone—had to be perfect. Ashley had been my rock, sneaking me food when my mother kept me on an eight-hundred calorie, no-carb diet. And talking to me so I wouldn't be scared or stir-crazy when Mother locked me in a completely black room so that I'd be forced to get my beauty sleep.

I'd thought she was together, and I'd drawn part of my strength from her. But when her husband left her and she killed herself because she'd believed she wasn't the person she should be, I knew that Mother had gotten in her head, too.

"I'm sorry," I whisper to her now. "I'm so sorry she screwed you up—hell, I'm sorry she screwed both of us up." I draw in a breath. "But I'm doing better. I think you'd be proud of me. I love you," I say. "And I miss you."

I wipe the tears from my eyes as I return the picture to the bureau. I meant what I said. I *am* doing better. I've been doing better ever since I moved out of my mother's house. But it wasn't until I met Damien that I truly felt like I was wriggling free of the quicksand in which my mother had buried me.

But now—with the laughter of my daughter echoing just outside the window—I know that I can be better still. And, I think, I finally know what I need to do.

It takes a few minutes for me to get all my ducks in order, but once I've thought it all through and made a couple of phone calls, I know that I'm on the right path. The knot in my stomach has disappeared, along with the band around my chest. I feel light and giddy, and as I hurry down the steps, I feel Damien's eyes on me and wave happily.

Lara is in the sandbox now, building something that I think is supposed to be a castle, but might be a horse, her current favorite animal.

I pause to give her a kiss and come away with my lips a little gritty. "Let me talk with Daddy," I say. "And I'll come back in a little bit, okay?"

"Okay, Mama," she says, then shoves her hands deep into a mountain of sand. I take a quick detour to peek at Anne, napping in the shade in her portable crib, then I head toward Damien.

"Feeling better?" Damien asks, moving over so that I can sit beside him on the edge of the hot tub and dangle my feet in the water.

"Yeah," I say, taking his hand. "Thanks."

"For what?"

I laugh. "Well, we could start with everything. But mostly for putting up with me lately."

He lifts our joined hands and kisses my knuckles. "It's hard. We've gone from two to four. Plus, there are diapers in the mix."

"True, that," I say, then kick my feet, splashing us both a little. "Ashley killed herself because she felt like she wasn't perfect."

My voice is low, barely a whisper, but I know from the way Damien stiffens beside me that he's heard every word.

"I know." His eyes move as he examines my face. "Is that how you feel?"

"Yes. No." I draw a breath. "Not anymore. I—"

I pull my hand free and run it through my hair, trying to organize in words the feelings—and the decision—that are so clear in my heart. "So here's the thing. I love designing my apps. The small challenges. And the large ones. Working out tricky code. Thinking up clever or funny or useful programs that will grab people's attention and give them a break or help them with productivity."

"And you're good at it."

"I am," I agree, because my talent and skill in my job is something I've never questioned. "And when I first wanted to go into business for myself, it was so that I could do what I wanted. Not what my boss said, or a client I didn't sign personally asked for."

"Control," he says dryly. "I get that."

I lean over and bump him with my shoulder. "Yeah, I'm sure you do."

I start to sit up straight again, but he hooks an arm around me. "And now you're overwhelmed because you've taken on something that's even bigger than the work—the business. You've got the coding that you love, and all the other bullshit that you don't."

"Payroll taxes and accounting and client development and all of it. Yes," I say, not at all surprised that he understands. Damien knows me well, after all. "But I don't want to give it up. I just want—"

"The core," he finishes for me.

I look at him, surprised by his choice of word. "Exactly. And I'm not sure whether I felt like I had to compete with you or if I was trying to prove what a success I was to my mother, or if I just didn't want to feel like I failed. But the truth is, I know I didn't. I have a great business, and I don't have to go at it a million miles an hour. Not when I can slow down and enjoy everything else I have." I take his hand again and squeeze as I look toward Lara and Anne.

"You've been doing a lot of thinking."

"Mostly in the back of my mind. It's been churning, I think, without me even really being aware. But it was when you asked me if I'd cut that everything clicked into place."

Again, he tenses beside me, and I press my hand onto his thigh. "It clicked in a good way," I explain. "With the cutting…well, I think I needed the blade when I was lost. When I couldn't see any other way around the pain or the fear and the mess of everything that overwhelmed me."

"But this time you didn't want to cut," he says softly.

"Didn't even think about it," I confirm. "Not even a tiny bit." I smile up at him. "Do you get it? It's because I already knew what to do. I just hadn't let myself think about it yet."

"And what are you going to do?"

"Step back," I say, firmly. "I want my business, but I don't want or need to be Stark International." I flash a grin toward my husband. "You have that covered pretty well."

"I appreciate your vote of confidence," he says, and I laugh.

"And I'm going to sell the office in Studio City," I say. That one's harder. Because Damien bought my original unit as a present one magical Christmas, but I know it's the right thing to do. "I'll reinvest, but in something closer. Santa Monica, maybe. Or even Malibu. And in the meantime…"

I trail off, looking toward the beach. "Actually, I was thinking I could use the bungalow as a temporary office."

"It's your beach house, baby. If that's what you want, I say go for it."

"It is. I can have the kids with me, or if they're in the main house with Bree, I can be home in two minutes." I draw in a breath. "I think I was hearing my mother's voice in my head. That I had to be perfect—and somehow I confused perfect with doing it all. And the truth is, I don't have to be either."

"No," he agrees, "you don't. But never forget that you're perfect for me."

"Ditto," I say, then sigh, feeling relieved and centered and happy.

"What about Abby and Marge?"

"I'll keep them on. We'll use the living room as office space, and they can both work from home part time. But about Abby—there's more I haven't told you. Because, well, I want time here. With you and the kids. And it's a lot to shoulder, running even a scaled-back business. Don't laugh," I say when he starts to smile. "I'm not you, and you have about a billion people working for you. And entrepreneurism doesn't flow in my veins. That's your shtick."

"It is," he agrees.

"And you're exceptional at it. But I want someone helping me shoulder the load. A different kind of help than I get from my husband," I add with a grin. "So I asked Abby if she wanted to be a partner," I continue. "Starting at ten percent, but working her way up to fifty." I hesitate a little as I look at him because usually I run my business decisions by Damien before I float them in the world. But this time, I'd called Abby before even coming down the stairs.

"I think that's a great idea. And Abby will be an asset. It gives her a stake and takes some of the pressure off you. And," he adds, with a definite edge of humor, "you still have Stark International as a client. And I hear that company is always growing. So that's got to be good for your bottom line."

"It is," I agree, grateful he understands. "I want to keep my business. I'm proud of it, and I love what I do. But not if it means I miss all of this." I glance toward Anne's bassinet, then smile at Lara, who's now toddling toward us, covered in sand.

"I don't need to be Stark International. I just want my work. Mostly," I add, leaning in close, "I just want you."

"You have me. Don't ever doubt it."

"I don't," I say. "And I have something for you."

I stand, then leave wet footprints as I pad across the pool deck to where I'd left a small paper bag on a table at the foot of the stairs. When I come back, I hold it out to Damien, who looks up at me, confused.

"Pick one," I say, shaking the bag and making the tiny squares of folded paper rustle.

He laughs, but complies and then opens it. "Road trip," he reads. He glances up at me. "Want to clarify that?"

"Nope." I grin. "But you'll find out what it means tomorrow."

Chapter 10

"You're not going to tell me where we're going?" Damien asks. It's just past eight in the morning, and Edward is driving us eastward on Interstate 10 in the limousine.

"Not a chance," I say, taking his now-empty champagne glass and making him a fresh mimosa from the OJ and champagne I had Edward stock in the limo's bar. "You're stuck with me until we get there."

"There being...?"

"Ha. Like I'd fall for that."

He chuckles. "Worth a try." He takes a sip of the mimosa, then slides it into one of the holders designed for stemware. "How about this—if you won't tell me where we're going, will you at least tell me where the girls are?"

I tilt my head as if considering. "Do you trust me?"

"Completely," he says.

"Good," I say. "And you'll find out where your daughters are soon enough."

"Soon," he repeats, sounding almost disappointed.

I frown. "What?"

He shrugs. "Just that it's hard to take advantage of all that a limo has to offer if the ride is that short."

I narrow my eyes. "You're being sneaky, aren't you?"

"Me?"

I point at him. "Don't act all innocent. You're trying to figure out where we're going by figuring out how long the ride is."

He holds up his hands. "I plead not guilty."

"Hmm." I finish refilling my own mimosa and then slide back across the seat to sit next to him. "Well, the truth is, that all of those advantages that a limo has to offer is one of the reasons we're taking it and not one of your toys." Damien owns an impressive collection of cars, and rarely turns down an opportunity to take one on the open road. This morning, however, I wanted Damien beside me, and his hands somewhere other than the wheel.

"Really?" he replies. "I'm intrigued."

"Good," I say casually, reaching over him to put my mimosa beside his. Then I climb onto his lap and kiss him lightly. "Because it occurred to me that making out like teenagers in the backseat would be a very fun way to pass the time until we get to where we're going."

I can tell he's about to answer, but I silence him with a kiss. Soft at first, then harder and deeper when his lips part and I can tease him with my tongue. Then harder still as I feel him harden between my legs. I'm straddling him, my knees on the leather car seat, and the crotch of my khaki shorts pressed against his jean-clad erection.

We kiss and fondle for miles, stroking each other, teasing each other. Letting the heat build and build until it's harder and harder to resist the lure of taking this all the way, even though resisting is exactly what I intend to do.

I'd planned this morning to be about the heat and excitement of being in each other's arms, of simply turning each other on. But like a teenager, I'm craving more. And when Damien's hand snakes up my shirt and tugs my breast free of my bra, I arch my back and moan with pleasure.

"Am I going to get to third base, Nikki?"

"Absolutely not," I say, even as I grind against him, my body on fire. "I'm not that kind of a girl."

But I know I'm going to lose that battle—and that even in the losing, I'll win. I can see the challenge all too clearly on his face. And if my game is not telling him where we're going, then his game is fucking me in the back of the limo.

The truth is, where Damien is concerned, I have little resistance. And when he slides his hand up the leg of my shorts and strokes the soft skin at the juncture of my thigh and pelvis, I just about lose my mind.

"Take them off," he demands, and though I know I should argue, I eagerly comply, stripping off the shorts and underwear as he unfastens his jeans and frees his cock. "On me," he demands, and I'm so wet, so ready, that I don't hesitate. I straddle him, then lower myself as he guides his cock inside me. I move slowly, teasing us both, but in the end neither of us can stand it, and when he grabs my hips and slams me down on him, I cry out in both relief and passion.

"That's it, baby," he says. "I want you to ride me."

I reach up, using the roof of the limo to balance as I thrust down over and over on his cock.

At the same time, he teases my clit with his finger, while his mouth closes over my breast, his teeth grazing over my sensitive nipples.

The feeling is incredible—like a wire of passion from my breast to my core—and I find a rhythm, letting the sensation build and build. Harder and faster and wilder and deeper until I really can't take it anymore. "Damien," I cry out, exploding all around him, then collapsing forward to cling to his neck as he continues to fuck me, finally exploding inside me while his arms hold me tight, and then whispering, "Dear God, baby. I love you."

We cling to each other for a few miles, and then clean up and get dressed again, and as I snuggle close, I have to admit that I'm glad these teenagers in the backseat went all the way, because I feel wonderful.

When we reach San Bernardino and turn off the highway toward the mountains, Damien says, "Hmmm," and I turn to look at him, my eyes wide and innocent.

"Something to say, Mr. Stark?"

"Not a thing. I still have absolutely no clue where we're going."

"Uh-huh." I laugh, because of course he knows. We're heading to our house in Lake Arrowhead, and when we arrive at the Alpine-style chateau, Damien looks at me and grins.

I shrug. "It's a getaway," I say. "I cleared my calendar. And I had Rachel clear yours. We're both free until Monday. And," I add with a grin, "there are two little girls waiting inside who are going to be very glad to see their daddy."

I'm right about the latter. As soon as we go through the door, Lara comes racing toward us calling *"Baba, Mama,"* and Damien scoops her into his arms as Bree passes me Anne.

"They were good on the drive?"

"Angels," she assures me. She drove here in Damien's Range Rover and is going back in the limo.

I cuddle Anne and remind Bree that Edward already knows the limo is at her disposal until we get back. "So do something fun. Have Edward take you and some friends on a jaunt."

"I don't know," she says, but her small grin makes me think she has something—or someone—in mind.

As soon as she's out the door, I turn to Damien and Lara. "Ready to go back out?"

Damien's brows raise, but I just shrug. "It's time for breakfast. And I'm thinking I know a little girl who might like a waffle."

The shopping area has a wonderful restaurant right on the lake with the best waffles in the world, in my opinion. Certainly good enough to satisfy my waffle-loving kid.

"Waffa! Waffa!" Lara squeals and starts clapping, getting so excited and squirmy that Damien has to put her down.

"Family weekend," I say with a shrug. "I thought we could spend the morning having breakfast, then maybe take one of the boat tours on the lake. Lara would get a kick out of that. But if you'd rather, we can make waffles here."

I'm a terrible cook, but Damien's not. Which means that Damien would make the waffles. But if he wants to stay in, I'm game.

But he shakes his head and puts his arm around me, gazing down at Anne's sweet face. "Nope," he says. "A day out with my girls sounds like heaven. So long as I get a night in with my wife."

"Absolutely, Mr. Stark," I say, then kiss him lightly.

It takes a little time to load the Range Rover up with all the baby paraphernalia, but soon we're on our way and unpacking it all over again in the parking lot for the Lake Arrowhead Village shops.

Damien pushes the double stroller, but only Anne is in it. Lara is skipping along, holding my hand and chattering on about everything.

When we reach the restaurant, the owner greets us warmly. "So good to see you again," he says, then adds. "I haven't yet met the children." He smiles at Lara, who boldly holds her hand out to shake, then clucks over Anne.

Finally, he aims a wide smile at me before turning to Damien. "You have a lovely family, Mr. Stark."

Damien squeezes my hand as he looks down at our girls. "Yes," he agrees. "I do."

THE END

* * * *

Also from 1001 Dark Nights and J. Kenner, discover Tame Me, Tempt Me, Caress of Darkness, and Caress of Pleasure.

Sign up for the 1001 Dark Nights Newsletter
and be entered to win a Tiffany Key necklace.

There's a contest every month!

Go to www.1001DarkNights.com to subscribe.

As a bonus, all subscribers will receive a free
1001 Dark Nights story
The First Night
by Lexi Blake & M.J. Rose

Turn the page for a full list of the
1001 Dark Nights fabulous novellas...

Discover 1001 Dark Nights Collection Four

Go to www.1001DarkNights.com for more information.

BLADE by Alexandra Ivy/Laura Wright
A Bayou Heat Novella

DRAGON BURN by Donna Grant
A Dark Kings Novella

TRIPPED OUT by Lorelei James
A Blacktop Cowboys® Novella

STUD FINDER by Lauren Blakely

MIDNIGHT UNLEASHED by Lara Adrian
A Midnight Breed Novella

HALLOW BE THE HAUNT by Heather Graham
A Krewe of Hunters Novella

DIRTY FILTHY FIX by Laurelin Paige
A Fixed Novella

THE BED MATE by Kendall Ryan
A Room Mate Novella

NIGHT GAMES by CD Reiss
A Games Novella

NO RESERVATIONS by Kristen Proby
A Fusion Novella

DAWN OF SURRENDER by Liliana Hart
A MacKenzie Family Novella

Discover 1001 Dark Nights Collection One

Go to www.1001DarkNights.com for more information.

FOREVER WICKED by Shayla Black
CRIMSON TWILIGHT by Heather Graham
CAPTURED IN SURRENDER by Liliana Hart
SILENT BITE: A SCANGUARDS WEDDING by Tina Folsom
DUNGEON GAMES by Lexi Blake
AZAGOTH by Larissa Ione
NEED YOU NOW by Lisa Renee Jones
SHOW ME, BABY by Cherise Sinclair
ROPED IN by Lorelei James
TEMPTED BY MIDNIGHT by Lara Adrian
THE FLAME by Christopher Rice
CARESS OF DARKNESS by Julie Kenner

Also from 1001 Dark Nights

TAME ME by J. Kenner

Discover 1001 Dark Nights Collection Two
Go to www.1001DarkNights.com for more information.

WICKED WOLF by Carrie Ann Ryan
WHEN IRISH EYES ARE HAUNTING by Heather Graham
EASY WITH YOU by Kristen Proby
MASTER OF FREEDOM by Cherise Sinclair
CARESS OF PLEASURE by Julie Kenner
ADORED by Lexi Blake
HADES by Larissa Ione
RAVAGED by Elisabeth Naughton
DREAM OF YOU by Jennifer L. Armentrout
STRIPPED DOWN by Lorelei James
RAGE/KILLIAN by Alexandra Ivy/Laura Wright
DRAGON KING by Donna Grant
PURE WICKED by Shayla Black
HARD AS STEEL by Laura Kaye
STROKE OF MIDNIGHT by Lara Adrian
ALL HALLOWS EVE by Heather Graham
KISS THE FLAME by Christopher Rice
DARING HER LOVE by Melissa Foster
TEASED by Rebecca Zanetti
THE PROMISE OF SURRENDER by Liliana Hart

Also from 1001 Dark Nights

THE SURRENDER GATE By Christopher Rice
SERVICING THE TARGET By Cherise Sinclair

Discover 1001 Dark Nights Collection Three

Go to www.1001DarkNights.com for more information.

HIDDEN INK by Carrie Ann Ryan
BLOOD ON THE BAYOU by Heather Graham
SEARCHING FOR MINE by Jennifer Probst
DANCE OF DESIRE by Christopher Rice
ROUGH RHYTHM by Tessa Bailey
DEVOTED by Lexi Blake
Z by Larissa Ione
FALLING UNDER YOU by Laurelin Paige
EASY FOR KEEPS by Kristen Proby
UNCHAINED by Elisabeth Naughton
HARD TO SERVE by Laura Kaye
DRAGON FEVER by Donna Grant
KAYDEN/SIMON by Alexandra Ivy/Laura Wright
STRUNG UP by Lorelei James
MIDNIGHT UNTAMED by Lara Adrian
TRICKED by Rebecca Zanetti
DIRTY WICKED by Shayla Black
THE ONLY ONE by Lauren Blakely
SWEET SURRENDER by Liliana Hart

About J. Kenner

J. Kenner (aka Julie Kenner) is the *New York Times*, *USA Today*, *Publishers Weekly*, *Wall Street Journal* and #1 International bestselling author of over eighty novels, novellas and short stories in a variety of genres.

JK has been praised by *Publishers Weekly* as an author with a "flair for dialogue and eccentric characterizations" and by *RT Bookclub* for having "cornered the market on sinfully attractive, dominant antiheroes and the women who swoon for them." A five-time finalist for Romance Writers of America's prestigious RITA award, JK took home the first RITA trophy awarded in the category of erotic romance in 2014 for her novel, *Claim Me* (book 2 of her Stark Trilogy).

In her previous career as an attorney, JK worked as a lawyer in Southern California and Texas. She currently lives in Central Texas, with her husband, two daughters, and two rather spastic cats.

Visit JK online at www.jkenner.com
Subscribe to JK's Newsletter
Text JKenner to 21000 to subscribe to JK's text alerts
Twitter
Instagram
Facebook Page
Facebook Fan Group

Discover More J. Kenner/Julie Kenner

Tempt Me: A Stark International Novella
By J. Kenner

Now Available

Sometimes passion has a price…

When sexy Stark Security Chief Ryan Hunter whisks his girlfriend Jamie Archer away for a passionate, romance-filled weekend so he can finally pop the question, he's certain that the answer will be an enthusiastic yes. So when Jamie tries to avoid the conversation, hiding her fears of commitment and change under a blanket of wild sensuality and decadent playtime in bed, Ryan is more determined than ever to convince Jamie that they belong together.

Knowing there's no halfway with this woman, Ryan gives her an ultimatum – marry him or walk away. Now Jamie is forced to face her deepest insecurities or risk destroying the best thing in her life. And it will take all of her strength, and all of Ryan's love, to keep her right where she belongs…

* * * *

Tame Me: A Stark International Novella
By J. Kenner

Now Available

Aspiring actress Jamie Archer is on the run. From herself. From her wild child ways. From the screwed up life that she left behind in Los Angeles. And, most of all, from Ryan Hunter—the first man who has the potential to break through her defenses to see the dark fears and secrets she hides.

Stark International Security Chief Ryan Hunter knows only one thing for sure—he wants Jamie. Wants to hold her, make love to her, possess her, and claim her. Wants to do whatever it takes to make her his.

But after one night of bliss, Jamie bolts. And now it's up to Ryan to not only bring her back, but to convince her that she's running away from the best thing that ever happened to her--him.

* * * *

Caress of Darkness: A Dark Pleasures Novella
By Julie Kenner

Now Available

From the first moment I saw him, I knew that Rainer Engel was like no other man. Dangerously sexy and darkly mysterious, he both enticed me and terrified me.

I wanted to run—to fight against the heat that was building between us—but there was nowhere to go. I needed his help as much as I needed his touch. And so help me, I knew that I would do anything he asked in order to have both.

But even as our passion burned hot, the secrets in Raine's past reached out to destroy us ... and we would both have to make the greatest sacrifice to find a love that would last forever.

Don't miss the next novellas in the Dark Pleasures series!

Find Me in Darkness, Find Me in Pleasure, Find Me in Passion, Caress of Pleasure...

* * * *

Storm, Texas.

Where passion runs hot, desire runs deep, and secrets have the power to destroy...

Nestled among rolling hills and painted with vibrant wildflowers, the bucolic town of Storm, Texas, seems like nothing short of perfection.

But there are secrets beneath the facade. Dark secrets. Powerful secrets. The kind that can destroy lives and tear families apart. The kind that can cut through a town like a tempest, leaving jealousy and destruction in its wake, along with shattered hopes and broken dreams. All it takes is one little thing to shatter that polish.

Rising Storm is a series conceived by Julie Kenner and Dee Davis to read like an on-going drama. Set in a small Texas town, Rising Storm is full of scandal, deceit, romance, passion, and secrets. Lots of secrets.

Wicked Grind

Stark World Novels, Book 1
By J. Kenner
Coming July 11, 2017

Sometimes it feels so damn good to be bad

Photographer Wyatt Royce's career is on the verge of exploding. All he needs is one perfect model to be the centerpiece of his sexy, controversial show. Find her, and Wyatt is sure to have a winner.

Then Kelsey Draper walks in. Stunning. Vibrant. And far too fragile for a project like this. Wyatt should know—after all, he remembers only too well how their relationship ended all those years ago.

Desperate for cash and frustrated with her good girl persona, Kelsey sets her sights on Wyatt's show. But only the show. Because she knows too well that Wyatt Royce is a danger to her heart.

But when Wyatt agrees to give her the job only if he has complete control—on camera and in his bed—Kelsey can't help but wonder if she's in too deep. Because how can a good girl like her ever be enough for a man like Wyatt?

All Wicked novels stand alone.

* * * *

Prologue

I'd thought he was out of my life forever. That all that remained of him was a memory, sharp and forbidden. Terrifying, yet tempting.
The one man who changed everything.
The one night that destroyed my world.
I told myself I was past it. That I could see him again and not feel that tug.

Not remember the hurt or the shame.
   That's what I believed, anyway.
   Honestly, I should have known better...

Chapter 1

He was surrounded by naked women, and he was bored out of his mind.

Wyatt Royce forced himself not to frown as he lowered his camera without taking a single shot. Thoughtfully, he took a step back, his critical eye raking over the four women who stood in front of him in absolutely nothing but their birthday suits.

Gorgeous women. Confident women. With luscious curves, smooth skin, bright eyes, and the kind of strong, supple muscles that left no doubt that each and every one of them could wrap their legs around a man and hold him tight.

In other words, each one had an erotic allure. A glow. A certain *je ne sais quoi* that turned heads and left men hard.

None of them, however, had it.

"Wyatt? You ready, man?"

Jon Paul's voice pulled Wyatt from his frustrated thoughts, and he nodded at his lighting director. "Sorry. Just thinking."

JP turned his back to the girls before flashing a wolfish grin and lowering his voice. "I'll bet you were."

Wyatt chuckled. "Down, boy." Wyatt had hired the twenty-three-year-old UCLA photography grad student as a jack-of-all-trades six months ago. But when JP had proven himself to be not only an excellent photographer, but also a prodigy with lighting, the relationship had morphed from boss/assistant to mentor/protégé before finally holding steady at friend/colleague.

JP was damn good at his job, and Wyatt had come to rely on him. But JP's background was in architectural photography. And the fact that the female models he faced every day were not only gorgeous, but often flat-out, one hundred percent, provocatively nude, continued to be both a fascination to JP and, Wyatt suspected, the cause of a daily cold shower. Or three.

Not that Wyatt could criticize. After all, he was the one who'd manufactured the sensual, erotic world in which both he and JP spent their days. For months, he'd lost himself daily inside this studio, locked in with a series of stunning women, their skin warm beneath his fingers as he gently positioned them for the camera. Women eager to please. To move however he directed. To contort their bodies in enticing, tantalizing poses that were often unnatural and uncomfortable, and for no other reason than that he told them to.

As long as they were in front of his camera, Wyatt owned those women, fully and completely. And he'd be lying to himself if he didn't admit that in many ways the photo shoots were as erotically charged as the ultimate photographs.

So, yeah, he understood the allure, but he'd damn sure never succumbed to it. Not even when so many of his models had made it crystal clear that they were eager to move from his studio to his bedroom.

There was just too much riding on this project.

Too much? Hell, everything was riding on his upcoming show. His career. His life. His reputation. Not to mention his personal savings.

Eighteen months ago he'd set out to make a splash in the world of art and photography, and in just twenty-seven days, he'd find out if he'd succeeded.

What he hoped was that success would slam against him like a cannonball hitting water. So hard and fast that everybody in the vicinity ended up drenched, with him squarely at the center, the unabashed cause of all the commotion.

What he feared was that the show would be nothing more than a ripple, as if he'd done little more than stick his big toe into the deep end of the pool.

Behind him, JP coughed, the harsh sound pulling Wyatt from his thoughts. He glanced up, saw that each of the four women were staring at him with hope in their eyes, and felt like the ultimate heel.

"Sorry to keep you waiting, ladies. Just trying to decide how I want you." He spoke without any innuendo, but the petite brunette giggled anyway, then immediately pressed her lips together and dipped her gaze to the floor. Wyatt pretended not to notice. "JP, go grab my Leica from my office. I'm thinking I want to shoot black and white."

He wasn't thinking that at all, not really. He was just buying time. Talking out of his ass while he decided what—if anything—to do with the girls.

As he spoke, he moved toward the women, trying to figure out why the hell he was so damned uninterested in all of them. Were they really that inadequate? So unsuited for the role he needed to fill?

Slowly, he walked around them, studying their curves, their angles, the soft glow of their skin under the muted lighting. This one had a haughty, aquiline nose. That one a wide, sensual mouth. Another had the kind of bedroom eyes that promised to fulfill any man's fantasies. The fourth, a kind of wide-eyed innocence that practically begged to be tarnished.

Each had submitted a portfolio through her agent, and he'd spent hours poring over every photograph. He had one slot left in the show. The centerpiece. The lynchpin. A single woman that would anchor all of his carefully staged and shot photos with a series of erotic images that he could already see clearly in his mind. A confluence of lighting and staging, of body and attitude. Sensuality coupled with innocence and underscored with daring.

He knew what he wanted. More than that, somewhere in the deep recesses of his mind, he even knew who he wanted.

So far, she hadn't wandered into his studio.

But she was out there, whoever she was; he was certain of it.

Too bad he only had twenty-seven days to find her.

Which was why he'd stooped to scouring modeling agencies, even though his vision for this show had always been to use amateur models. Women whose features or attitude caught his attention on the beach, in the grocery store, wherever he might be. Women from his past. Women from his work. But always women who didn't make a living with their bodies. That had been his promise to himself from the beginning.

And yet here he was, begging agents to send their most sensual girls to him. Breaking his own damn rule because he was desperate to find her. That elusive girl who was hiding in his mind, and who maybe—just maybe—had an agent and a modeling contract.

But he knew she wouldn't. Not that girl.

No, the girl he wanted would be a virgin with the camera, and he'd be the one who would first capture that innocence. That was his vision. The plan he'd stuck to for eighteen long months of squeezing in sessions between his regular commercial photography gigs. Almost two years of all-nighters in the dark room and surviving on coffee and protein bars because there wasn't time to order take-out, much less cook.

Months of planning and worrying and slaving toward a goal. And those sweet, precious moments when he knew—really knew—that he was on the verge of creating something truly spectacular.

He was exhausted, yes. But he was almost done.

So far, he had forty-one final images chosen for the show, each and every one perfect as far as he was concerned.

He just needed the final nine. That last set of photos of his one perfect woman. Photos that would finally seal his vision—both of the girl in his mind and of what he wanted to accomplish with this solo exhibition.

He'd sacrificed so much, and he was finally close. So damn close... And yet here he was, spinning his wheels with models who weren't what he wanted or needed.

Fuck.

With a sigh of frustration, Wyatt dragged his fingers through his thick, short hair. "Actually, ladies, I think we're done here. I appreciate your time and your interest in the project, and I'll review your portfolios and be in touch with your agent if you're selected. You're free to get dressed and go."

The girls glanced at each other, bewildered. For that matter, JP looked equally puzzled as he returned to the studio with Wyatt's Leica slung over his shoulder and a tall, familiar redhead at his side.

"Siobhan," Wyatt said, ignoring the trepidation building in his gut. "I didn't realize we had a meeting scheduled."

"I thought you were going to shoot a roll of black and white," JP said at the same time, holding up the Leica in the manner of a third grader at Show-and-Tell.

In front of Wyatt, the girls paused in the act of pulling on their robes, obviously uncertain.

"We're done," Wyatt said to them before turning his attention to his assistant. "I have everything I need to make a decision."

"Right. Sure. You're the boss." But as JP spoke, he looked sideways at Siobhan, whose arms were now crossed over her chest, her brow furrowed with either confusion or annoyance. Quite probably both.

But Wyatt had to hand it to her; she held in her questions until the last model had entered the hallway that led to the dressing room, and the door had clicked shut behind her.

"You got what you needed?" she asked, cutting straight to the chase. "Does that mean one of those models is the girl you've been looking for?"

"Is that why you're here? Checking my progress?" Shit. He sounded like a guilty little boy standing in front of the principal.

Siobhan, thank God, just laughed. "One, I'm going to assume from the defensive tone that the answer is no. And two, I'm the director of your show first and foremost because we're friends. So take this in the spirit of friendship when I ask, what the hell are you doing? We have less than a month to pull all of this together. So if none of those girls is the one you need, then tell me what I can do to help. Because this is on me, too, remember? This show flops, and we both lose."

"Thanks," he said dryly. "I appreciate the uplifting and heartfelt speech."

"Screw uplifting. I want you on the cover of every art and photography magazine in the country, with your show booked out on loan to at least a dozen museums and galleries for the next five years. I couldn't care less if you're uplifted. I just want you to pull this off."

"Is that all?" he asked, fighting a smile.

"Hell no. I also want a promotion. My boss is considering moving to Manhattan. I covet her office."

"Good to have a goal," JP said, tilting his head toward Wyatt. "I covet his."

"Go," Wyatt said, waving his thumb toward the dressing room. "Escort the girls out through the gallery," he ordered. The space was divided into his two-story studio that boasted a discreet entrance off the service alley, and a newly remodeled gallery and storefront that opened onto one of Santa Monica's well-trafficked retail areas.

"So you're really done?" JP pressed. "That's it? Not even a single shot?"

"I don't need to see anything else," Wyatt said. "Go. Chat them up so they don't feel like they wasted their time. And then I'll see you tomorrow."

"That's your subtle way of getting rid of me, isn't it?"

"Don't be ridiculous," Wyatt retorted. "I wasn't being subtle at all."

JP smirked, but didn't argue. And with a wave to Siobhan, he disappeared into the back hallway.

"So how can I help?" Siobhan asked once he was gone. "Should I arrange a round of auditions? After all, I know a lot of really hot women."

That was true enough. In fact, Siobhan's girlfriend, Cassidy, featured prominently in the show. And it had been through Cass that Wyatt had originally met Siobhan, who had both a background in art and a shiny new job as the assistant director of the Stark Center for the Visual Arts in downtown Los Angeles.

Originally, Wyatt had envisioned a significantly smaller show staged in his studio. The location was good, after all, and he anticipated a lot of foot traffic since folks could walk from the Third Street Promenade. He'd asked Cass to model about eight months ago, not only because she was stunning, but because he knew the flamboyant tattoo artist well enough to know that she wouldn't balk at any pose he came up with, no matter how provocative. Cass didn't have a shy bone in her body, and she was more than happy to shock—so long as the shock was delivered on her terms.

Siobhan had come with her, and before the shoot, Wyatt had shown both of them three of the pieces he'd already finished so that Cass would have a sense of his vision. It was the first time he'd laid it out in detail, and it had been cathartic talking to Siobhan, who spoke the language, and Cass, who was an artist herself, albeit one whose canvas was skin and whose tools were ink and needles.

He'd explained how he'd originally just wanted a break from the portraits and other commercial photography jobs that paid the bills. And, yes, he was beginning to make a name for himself artistically with his landscapes and city scenes. That success was gratifying, but ultimately unsatisfying because those subjects weren't his passion. There was beauty in nature, sure, but Wyatt wanted to capture physical, feminine eroticism on film.

More than that, he wanted to make a statement, to tell a story. Beauty. Innocence. Longing. Ecstasy. He wanted to look at the world through the eyes of these women, and the women through the eyes of the world.

Ultimately, he wanted to elevate erotic art. To use it to reveal more about the models than even they were aware. Strength and sensuality. Innocence and power. Passion and gentleness. He envisioned using a series of provocative, stunning images to manipulate the audience through the story of the show, sending them on a journey from innocence to debauchery and back again, and then leaving them breathless with desire and wonder.

That afternoon, Wyatt spoke with Cass and Siobhan for over an hour. Showing them examples. Describing the emotions he wanted to evoke. Listening to their suggestions, and taking satisfaction from the fact that they obviously loved the concept. They'd ended the conversation with Cass posing for another hour as he burned through three rolls of film, certain he was capturing some of his best work yet.

Then they'd walked to Q, a Santa Monica restaurant and bar known for its martini flights. They'd toasted his project, Cass's pictures, and Siobhan's career, and by the time they ended the evening, he was feeling pretty damn good about his little pet project.

The next morning, he'd felt even better. That's when Siobhan had come to him with a formal offer from the Stark Center. He'd said yes on the spot, never once thinking that by doing so he was tying another person to his success—or, more to the point, his potential failure.

"I'm serious," she pressed now, as his silence continued to linger. "Whatever you need."

"I'll find her," Wyatt said. "I have time."

"Not much," she countered. "I need the prints ahead of time for the catalog, not to mention installation. Keisha's already getting twitchy," she added, referring to her boss. "We don't usually cut it this close."

"I know. It's going to be—"

"Twenty-seven days to the show, Wyatt." He could hear the tension in her voice, and hated himself for being the cause of it. "But about half that before you need to deliver the prints. We're running out of time. If you can't find the girl, then you need to just find a girl. I'm sorry, but—"

"I said I'll find her. You have to trust me on this."

Right then, she didn't look like she'd trust him to take care of her goldfish, but to her credit, she nodded. "Fine. In that case, all I need today is to see the latest print so I can think about the promotional image. And you'll email me a file for the catalog?"

"Sure. This is it," he added, walking to a covered canvas centered on the nearest wall. He pulled down the white drape, revealing a life-size black and white photograph of a woman getting dressed. At first glance, it wasn't the most titillating of his images, but that was because it was such a tease. The woman stood in a dressing room, and hidden among the dresses and coats were at least a dozen men, peering out to watch her.

The woman, however, was oblivious. She was bending over, one foot on a stool as she fastened a garter. The view was at an angle, so at first glance the audience saw only her skirt, a hint of garter, and the woman's silk-sheathed leg.

Then they noticed the mirror behind her. A mirror that revealed that she wasn't wearing panties under the garter belt. And even though absolutely nothing was left to the imagination, it still wasn't a particularly racy or erotic photograph. But then you noticed the reflection in the mirror of another mirror. And another. And another. Each with an image of that same woman, and each slightly more risqué, until finally, as the mirror approached infinity, the woman was nude, her head thrown back, one hand between her legs, the other at her throat. And all those men from the closet were out in the open now, their hands stroking and teasing her.

Most important, the mirror was so deep in the image that you had to stand practically nose-to-print to see it.

Wyatt couldn't wait to see how many people did exactly that at the showing.

"This is fabulous," Siobhan said with genuine awe in her voice.

"It was a hell of a photograph to set up and then develop. Lots of work on the set and in the darkroom."

"You could have set it up digitally."

He scoffed. "No. Some of the images, sure. But not this one." He turned his head, regarding it critically. "This one had to be hands-on. It's as much about the process as the product."

"Yeah. I get that." She met his eyes, and the respect in hers reminded him of why he didn't just take photos for himself. "I want to take it back with me right now and show Keisha," she added.

"Soon." Although Siobhan and Keisha had wanted him to deliver each print upon completion, Wyatt had balked, explaining that he needed the art surrounding him in order to ensure the continuity of story in the overall exhibit. And the size of the canvas and the particulars of the way he handled the image in the darkroom were such that duplicates weren't adequate.

That meant that when Siobhan needed to see a piece, she came to him. And now that she was not only putting together the official catalog, but also doing promotional pieces from the images, she was coming a lot.

Wyatt was adamant that the images not be revealed prior to the show, but Siobhan's team had promised him the rapidly expanding catalog mockup would be kept under lock and key. More important, the pre-show promotion wouldn't reveal any of the artwork—while at the same time teasing the art's sensual and daring nature.

So far, they'd not only managed to do just that, but the campaign was already a success. The gallery had been releasing one image a month—one of his photographs, yes, but only a sexy snippet shown through a virtual barrier laid over the image. Once, it was yellow caution tape. Another time, it was a keyhole in a hotel room door. Clever, yes, but also effective. Wyatt had already been interviewed and the exhibit pimped out in no less than five local papers and magazines. And he was booked on two morning shows the day the exhibit opened.

Not bad, all things considered, and he told Siobhan as much.

"If you really want to see a bump in our publicity," she replied, "we should get your grandmother on board."

"No." The word came swift and firm.

"Wyatt..."

"I said no. This exhibit is on my shoulders. I can't hide who I am, but I don't have to advertise it. If we trot my grandmother out, book her on morning shows, make her sing little Wyatt's praises, then everyone is going to come. You know that."

"Um, yeah. That's the point. To get people to your show."

"I want them to come for the show. Not because they're hoping to get Anika Segel's autograph."

"But they'll see your art. They'll fall in love then. Who cares what brings them through the door?"

"I do," he said and was relieved to see that she didn't seem to have an argument against that.

She stood still for a moment, possibly trying to come up with something, but soon enough she shook her head and sighed. "You're the artist." She made a face. "And you have the temperament to go with it."

"See, that's how you wooed me into doing the show with you. That embarrassingly sentimental flattery."

"You're a laugh a minute, Wyatt." She hitched her purse farther onto her shoulder, then pointed a finger at him. "Don't fuck this up."

"Cross my heart."

"All right then." She leaned in for an air kiss, but caught him in a hug. "It's going to be great," she whispered, and he was surprised by how much he appreciated those simple words.

"It will," he agreed. "All I have to do is find the girl." He glanced at his watch. "An agency's sending someone over in about half an hour. Nia. Mia. Something like that. Who knows? Maybe she'll be the one."

"Fingers crossed." Her grin turned wicked. "But if she's not, just say the word and Cass and I will dive into the search."

"A few more days like today, and I'll take you up on that."

"A few days is all you have," she retorted, then tossed up her hands, self-defense style. "I know, I know. I'm leaving."

She headed for the front door, and he turned back to the print, studying it critically. A moment later he reached for the drapes that covered the prints on either side of the first image, then tugged them off, revealing the full-color photos beneath.

He took a step back as he continued his inspection, ensuring himself that there were no more refinements to be made. Slowly, he moved farther back, wanting all three in his field of vision, just like a visitor to the exhibition would see. One step, then another and another.

He stopped when he heard the door open behind him, cursing himself for not locking up as Siobhan was leaving. "Did you forget something?" he asked as he turned.

But it wasn't Siobhan.

It was her.

The girl who'd filled his mind. The girl who'd haunted his nights.

The woman he needed if he was going to pull this exhibit off the way he wanted to.

A woman with the kind of wide sensual mouth that could make a man crazy, and a strong, lithe body, with curves in all the right places. Eyes that could see all the way into a man's soul—and an innocent air that suggested she wouldn't approve of what she saw there.

All of that, topped off with a wicked little tease of a smile and a sexy swing to her hips.

She was a walking contradiction. Sensual yet demure. Sexy yet sweet.

A woman who one minute could look like a cover model, and the next like she'd never done anything more glamorous than walk the dog.

She was hotter than sin, and at the same time she was as cold as ice.

She was Kelsey Draper, and he hadn't spoken to her since the summer before his senior year, and as far as he was concerned, that was a damn good thing.

Her eyes widened as she looked at him, and her lips twitched in a tremulous smile. "Oh," was all she said.

And in that moment, Wyatt knew that he was well and truly screwed.

On behalf of 1001 Dark Nights,

Liz Berry and M.J. Rose would like to thank ~

Steve Berry
Doug Scofield
Kim Guidroz
Jillian Stein
InkSlinger PR
Dan Slater
Asha Hossain
Chris Graham
Pamela Jamison
Fedora Chen
Kasi Alexander
Jessica Johns
Dylan Stockton
Richard Blake
BookTrib After Dark
and Simon Lipskar

Made in the USA
San Bernardino, CA
18 July 2018